DARK MATTER
The Order of the Hidden Cross

IAN BAYLY

The Shadows Are Stirring

ASHLAR
PRESS

ISBN: 9781764298308

Published by Ashlar Press
www.AshlarPress.com
info@AshlarPress.com

Author Contact:
www.ianbayly.com
contact@ianbayly.com
Facebook & Instagram: @ianbayly.author
Patreon.com/ianbayly

I've Got an Idea Pty Ltd T/a Ashlar Press
ABN: 97 676 078 943

Disclaimer:

10 9 8 7 6 5 4 3

For Kim

Contents

(uncouth) Forward
By Ian Bayly

Forewords are usually written by someone *(in)*famous—an accomplished author, a critic who's read more books than I've had hot dinners, or maybe a minor celebrity who once played a corpse in a crime drama. The kind of person who can say, "Trust me, this book is worth your time," with a straight face. Sadly, I don't know any of those people. Honestly, I'm not even sure my own friends would lie for me. So, it's just me, Ian Bayly, doing the honours.

If you're wondering, "Is this allowed? Can he write his own foreword?" the answer is technically no. But when there is nobody else around, you get to bend a few rules. Think of it like eating cake for breakfast when no one's around to judge you—or, in my case, eating cake for breakfast because no one else is around at all. I'm writing my own introduction because Ian does what Ian wants, and really, who's going to stop me?

Writing "Dark Matter" was a bit like wandering through a haunted house—sometimes thrilling, sometimes confusing, and frequently making me question my life choices. For the forward, you're supposed to have someone who knows you well explain to the reader how the author overcame great obstacles, suffered for their art, and ultimately emerged triumphant. But let's be real: I didn't conquer my demons; I invited them in, made them a cup of tea, and they've been hanging around ever since, living in my head rent free and making sarcastic comments when I'm trying to work. If you were hoping for an inspiring tale of perseverance, well, you're definitely in the wrong place. This book was born out of late-night conversations with my personal darkness, where we'd swap stories, make terrible decisions, and occasionally stare into the abyss until it stared back—except the abyss didn't just stare; it winked and whispered, "I've got an idea!"

What's "Dark Matter" about, you ask? Well, it's a bit like life: dark, a bit messy, occasionally funny, and full of questionable themes. Imagine the sort of existential crisis that creeps up on you around 2 a.m. when you're lying in bed, staring at the ceiling, and seriously considering whether or not you should just disappear into the woods and live off canned beans for the rest of your life. It's that feeling but on paper. I wrote this book during a time when things were... let's just say, not going great. Not the kind of "not great" where you turn to your favourite comfort show and eat an entire pizza in one sitting, but more the kind where you find yourself seeking answers to questions you have not even thought about yet. Mind spinning so fast you can't even tell it's spinning.

Look, I'm not going to pretend "Dark Matter" is a literary masterpiece. Nor can I promise you'll love it. Hell, I can't even promise it'll make sense. But if you're into dark themes, a bit of existential dread, and metaphors that punch you in the gut when you least expect it, then welcome aboard!

And if you were hoping for a foreword written by a literary icon, just close your eyes and imagine I'm one of those mysterious, reclusive authors who never leave their mansion except to deliver cryptic quotes in interviews that end up as viral posts on social media. If it helps, picture me as the kind of person who'd write at a dusty old desk by candlelight, even though there's perfectly good electricity, because it makes the shadows dance just right.

So, if you're still here and not already regretting your decision to pick up this book, I'll say this: grab a drink *(perhaps something strong)*, find a comfortable spot, and settle in. We're going to explore some dark corners together, and maybe we'll find a few new demons along the way—probably the kind you shouldn't admit exist in polite company, but who cares? It's just us here. Right?

Welcome to "Dark Matter." It's strange, chaotic, and definitely a little unhinged, but so am I. And if you've stuck around this long, maybe you are too. In which case, I think we're going to get along just fine. *Tea?*

"*He who fights with monsters should be careful lest he thereby become a monster. And if you gaze long enough into an abyss, the abyss will gaze back into you.*"

Nietzsche
Beyond Good and Evil.

Chapter 1

The Night of Shadows and Storms

The baby's first cry split the night like a war horn, a sound too fierce, too primal to belong to a newborn. The village of Kul lay submerged in darkness, cloaked in a thick, oppressive blackness that stretched out like a suffocating blanket. The rain, relentless and cold, came down in sheets, turning the ground to slick mud, as though the earth itself was sinking under the weight of something ancient and terrible.

Joshua came into the world wet, screaming, and covered in blood and afterbirth. His voice pierced the night, too loud, too wild, a cry not of life, but of defiance. His mother, Zivah, lay on the muddy roadside, clutching him to her chest, desperate to quiet him. Fear surged in her chest as the world seemed to press in around her, the shadows watching, waiting. The more he cried, the more the night stirred.

But the baby would not be silenced.

Thunder rolled in the distance, but there was no comfort in its sound. The storm was no ordinary storm either. The rain did not fall to nourish or cleanse; it fell like daggers from the sky, cold and sharp, each drop biting into her skin. How much longer could she endure this? Every drop felt like a judgment, like the world itself was rebelling against her child. The wind howled like a wounded animal, shrieking through the trees with a voice full of rage, full of warning. The night itself felt alive, crawling with unseen things that moved just beyond the edge of vision, hidden but present, lurking beneath every shadow.

We watched them.

You might be wondering who 'We' are, and it is only fair that you know who is telling you this tale…

We are the unspoken, the unseen. We are the keepers of all secrets, all thoughts, all memories. We are your desires, your regrets, your fantasies, and your nightmares. We are the Memory Keepers, and our task is simple: to remember. We are your indictment, the eternal witnesses to your deeds, your sins, your hidden truths. We do not judge, but We do not forget.

This account is not just about a child. It is about a child who knew too much about Us. A child who knew how to manipulate Us. We do not like to admit this, but We cannot lie. We are everything you think, everything you dream, everything you wish to hide, as beautiful and as ugly as it may be. And this memory, this one tale, is important for you to know. Those who do not remember their history are bound to repeat it… so do with it what you will.

Zivah's breath came shallow and quick. She was alone, on the side of a road, a screaming child in her arms, and a growing sense of dread creeping over her. The sky above her was a roiling mass of black clouds, thick and churning like smoke from a great fire. No stars shone down upon her, no light pierced the heavy veil of the storm. The moon, once full and bright, had been swallowed by the darkness, leaving her stranded in a world that no longer felt her own.

Her mind drifted to Asher—the man who left when she needed him most. Three months pregnant, and he couldn't accept her truth. Or maybe she couldn't accept it herself. A good man by all accounts—

steady job, reliable—until the news that she carried a child shattered everything. But it wasn't Asher's abandonment that haunted her now. It was the child she'd given birth to—the child who shouldn't be here.

"It was all a dream," she had told Asher, tears in her eyes, pleading. "I swear, it was just a dream." But Asher had not believed her. He couldn't. And Zivah wasn't sure if she believed herself.

We remember that night.

We remember everything. For We are the unseen witnesses to all that has been and all that will be. We are your thoughts, your desires, your regrets. We hold your secrets—those you have hidden even from yourself. We do not judge, but We remember. And so, We have come to remember him.

The wind carried with it the stench of rot, damp earth, and something else—something older, fouler. It was the scent of decay, of things long buried in the depths of the earth, things that should never have seen the light of day. Whispers echoed through the trees, voices that belonged to neither man nor beast. They slithered through the air like serpents, curling around her, crawling beneath her skin.

Zivah's eyes darted around, heart pounding in her chest. The rain offered no comfort. The darkness felt thick, almost tangible, like it could swallow her whole. Every tree looked gnarled, twisted, as if straining toward her, stretching skeletal branches out to pluck the life from her. Flesh-eaters roam here, she thought, trying to still her son's cries, but she could not still her own terror. Her mind raced, filled with images of fangs and claws hidden in the gloom, waiting for the right moment to strike.

Zivah looked eastward. The storm was building, a violent, living thing. Black clouds blotted out the horizon, flickering with sickly green lightning, casting the world in eerie flashes that made the trees look like jagged teeth. She tried to calm herself, to soothe her child, but her thoughts returned to those dark memories she couldn't shake. Three months pregnant, Asher had left her. Three months pregnant, and she swore no man had ever touched her. Her body, swelling with life, waged war against her own understanding while a storm of fragmented memories lashed at her mind—each shadowed whisper more chilling than the last, hinting at truths too terrifying to grasp.

But now, in the dead of night, that mystery seemed small compared to the things she sensed closing in.

The air around her thickened with an unnatural chill. Shadows began to move with purpose. Zivah blinked, certain her mind was playing tricks on her, but the dark shapes continued to shift, edging closer. Creatures—grotesque and impossible—slithered out of the blackness, their translucent forms pulsating with an unnatural glow, wings like torn parchment rustling in the storm's wind. Some with horns, some with eyes like hollow voids. Their forms rippled as if they were made of the night itself, as if they were stitched together from pieces of the darkness. They moved between the trees, merging with the gloom, but she could feel them. Their gaze was not on her. It was on the child.

They had come to see him.

A particularly ghastly one, a beast of many eyes and wings like torn parchment, hovered near. Zivah's breath caught in her throat, her body trembling. She pressed her back against the nearest tree, desperate to hide, desperate for protection, but there was none. Her body had given all it could in the birth, and now it left her weak. She was too close to Death, closer than she had ever been.

We watched her, but We did not interfere. We do not control the threads of fate; we only watch as they unravel. But the Others—they did not come to harm. They too came to witness.

Zivah's mind swirled with confusion and fear. I must be dying, she thought. I'm hallucinating, I must be... She began to faint, consciousness slipping, when one of the creatures—a being of impossible size and form—came closer. It loomed over her, its breath like ice on her skin. It leaned in, close enough to pierce her with its hollow eyes, and whispered something ancient, something that froze her bones and stilled her heart.

At that very moment, a lightning bolt violently crashed down upon them, piercing into her very soul. The words spoken by the creature filled her with a sudden and powerful surge of energy, a healing force from the old ways, one that she desperately needed. It was as though the earth itself had lent its strength, weaving her back from the brink of death.

We should note that this type of magic comes at a great personal cost to the one who speaks it. This incantation is not something to be uttered lightly. For with every word, the speaker relinquishes part of their existence—an irreversible sacrifice. Once spoken, they are lost to the realms beyond this world, gone forever. This creature, for all its darkness, has given the last of itself to save her.

The creature pulled away, its monstrous eyes still fixed on the child. The other beings, now more like shadows than forms, watched from the edges of the world. They knew the risks. They had seen this before.

Did it work?
      I think so.
            We'll soon find out.

Zivah collapsed into a deep sleep.

Without warning another bolt of lightning crashed from the heavens, striking the earth just feet away, lighting the scene in a brief, violent flash. The creature, the monstrous thing that had whispered to her, vanished. In its place, the others circled the child, whispering, murmuring, paying tribute.

Joshua opened his eyes, their gaze sharper than any newborn's. The guttural sounds he made were no cries—they were commands. And the creatures bowed, shadows folding low, as if before their sovereign.

We knew then what he was. He spoke with authority beyond his years, beyond time. He spoke with the knowledge of the Forgotten, those banished to the space between life and death. He spoke to Us, and We listened.

By the time Zivah woke, the beasts had retreated to the shadows. Her vision blurred, her body felt like it was no longer hers. Was it a dream? she wondered. The memory felt strange, distant, as though the world itself had shifted in her absence. But no—there were footprints in the mud, strange, inhuman footprints, and the storm had calmed.

The baby stirred in her arms, no longer crying. The world was silent. Too silent.

Suddenly, three figures emerged from the darkness, hunched over, squinting through the rain. They were human, that much Zivah could tell, but her heart still raced. Could they be trusted?

"Miss! Are you alright? We thought we heard a baby out here!" one of the men shouted.

As they approached, Zivah could make out their faces—three rough-looking men, soaked from the storm. The one who spoke, Luke, crouched by her side. "I'm a doctor," he said, looking at the baby still attached by the umbilical cord. "Let me help you."

Simon, the second man, squinted at her through the rain. "Bloody hell, she's just given birth right out here on the street." He glanced at the baby, still covered in muck. "That one's got a set of lungs on him."

"Simon, stop gawking and go get my medical bag," Luke snapped, not taking his eyes off Zivah. "We need to get her cleaned up before infection sets in."

Simon grumbled under his breath as he turned to run back to the house. "Fucking kids… Always at the worst time."

The third man, Tom, stood awkwardly, shifting his weight from foot to foot. "What do we do now? I've never… you know… done this."

"Grab some towels and help me clean the baby," Luke instructed as he worked quickly, cutting the umbilical cord. The moment the cord was severed, a strange stillness settled over them. The rain stopped mid-air, the wind fell silent, and the baby let out a single, piercing scream.

Tom stared at the child, his hands trembling. "Did you… did you see that? It's like the storm responded to him."

Soon after, Simon returned, out of breath, holding the medical bag. He stumbled backwards, his voice breaking. 'That kid… what the hell is he? It's like… like he's not human.

The baby fell silent, its eyes fixing on Simon with an intensity that made his breath catch. Simon staggered back, his face pale. "What the hell…? It's like he's looking through me."

Luke didn't answer. He worked with methodical precision, but even he couldn't shake the feeling that something was terribly wrong. "Let's get her cleaned up and get them inside. We'll figure this out later."

Zivah's breathing grew shallow, her body suddenly tense. She grimaced and gasped, clutching her stomach. "It's… it's still inside me…," she murmured, her face pale with exhaustion and pain.

Luke's expression darkened as he glanced down. "The placenta?… it hasn't been delivered yet." His hands moved quickly, pressing down on Zivah's abdomen, trying to help her expel it.

Zivah let out a groan of agony. The pressure was unbearable. She felt her insides shift, felt something tugging at her core. Her body, already weak, protested violently, but it wasn't over yet.

"Stay with me, Zivah," Luke said, his voice low but urgent. "You have to push. One more time. You need to get it out."

Zivah's grip tightened on the baby as she braced herself for one final push. The world around her spun, the darkness deepening, and the whispers returned—harsher now, darker, as if the earth itself demanded a price for the child she had birthed.

She clenched her teeth, her entire body convulsing with effort. A sudden gush of blood and fluids followed, and the placenta slipped out in a sickening, wet mass. Tom flinched at the sight, his face pale, while Simon turned away, muttering something under his breath.

"There you go," Luke said, his voice softening. "It's done."

Zivah collapsed back, gasping for breath, her vision blurry. The shadows around them seemed to pull back, receding, satisfied for the moment.

But the air still hummed with a strange tension, and though the storm had lessened, the sky above them remained black, as if the night itself was waiting—watching.

The baby stirred in her arms, no longer crying but awake. His eyes gleamed in the darkness, sharp and aware, far too aware for a newborn.

"Joshua," Zivah whispered, barely able to speak. "His name is Joshua. Joshua Carpenter"

Tom glanced down at the baby, who now wore an odd, knowing smile. "Joshua Carpenter, huh? Weird choice…"

"Just help me with the towels, Tom," Luke muttered, shaking his head.

The beasts that had watched from the shadows retreated further, unseen by the men. But Zivah saw them. And so did Joshua.

We did not interfere, but We knew then—this child would not walk the path of mortals. And the night had only begun to tell its story.

Chapter 2

Caius & Flavius

"I don't like it down here," Flavius muttered to himself, his voice barely breaking the silence within the dim corridor. His eyes darted to the shadows where the torchlight couldn't reach, as though expecting something to step out. The torches flickered weakly, their flames sputtering against the damp, stale air. The shadows stretched unnaturally, warping across the cold stone walls as if alive.

Caius scoffed, his fingers brushing the hilt of his blade. "Then maybe you're not cut out for this, Flavius. Caius stepped closer, his voice dropping to a whisper. "You think I like this any more than you? If we fail, it won't just be us down here." His voice carried the weight of practised indifference, but the faint tremor in his grip betrayed him.

Flavius' hand tightened around his blade, the weight of something unspoken pressing on him. "No, it's not the place," he whispered, his eyes drifting toward the locked door ahead.

"It's what's behind that door. The way it hums... like it's breathing. I think it's waking up."

Caius' eyes narrowed, a flicker of doubt crossing his face before he brushed it off with a cold laugh. "That's what they all say."

A sudden thud echoed from the other side of the door, low and deliberate, like a heartbeat. Caius froze, his dismissive grin fading. For once, he had nothing to say.

Chapter 3

Zivah's Dream

The warmth of the evening lingered in the air as Zivah sat beside Asher inside her family's tent. The soft glow from oil lamps cast flickering shadows on the intricately woven rugs that lined the floor, with the vibrant patterns dancing like whispers of forgotten stories. The thick canvas walls of the tent, adorned with tapestries, rustled gently in the breeze—a reminder of the vast plains stretching beyond. The scent of spiced lamb, dates, and fresh bread still clung to the air, a comforting memory of the evening meal they had shared.

Zivah's parents sat close by, sipping the last of their tea. Her mother had since retired to a quieter corner of the tent, stitching patterns into a piece of fabric by dim light, her focus elsewhere. This left Zivah, Asher, and her father lingering in conversation. Though her father's sharp eyes followed the crackling fire in the central pit, Zivah knew he was still paying close attention to every word exchanged between her and Asher.

For several months now, Zivah and Asher had been engaged. Despite the familiarity of their courtship, an air of formality still settled over them whenever her father was present. Asher, ever respectful, sat with his back straight, hands resting in his lap. But every now and then, he glanced at Zivah, his eyes warm and soft, which softened the edges of the stiff posture he held in front of her father.

When Zivah caught his gaze, she smiled, her pulse quickening in the intimacy of the moment. There was a silent promise in Asher's eyes—a shared understanding that they would soon be alone. Her heart fluttered with anticipation.

Sensing the unspoken exchange, her father cleared his throat, leaning forward to refill his teacup. "It's getting late," he remarked, his voice low yet commanding. His gaze shifted to Asher, and his tone carried the subtle weight of authority. "I think it's time you made your way home. Zivah has her own preparations for the night."

Asher's smile faltered briefly but quickly recovered. He nodded, always the respectful guest. "Of course, sir," he said as he rose to his feet. Turning to Zivah, his eyes lingered on hers for a moment longer. In a whisper meant only for her, he said, "I'll see you tomorrow." His voice carried a quiet excitement, as though the time they would spend apart would be fleeting.

Zivah's heart swelled as she watched him cross the soft rugs toward the entrance of the tent. Her father followed, nodding once as Asher stepped into the cool night air. The heavy flap of the tent fell shut behind him with a soft thud, leaving Zivah in the familiar warmth of her home. Her father paused for a brief moment, his eyes meeting hers before disappearing behind one of the inner fabric partitions to join her mother for the night.

Now, with the tent hushed, a different stillness settled in the air. The fire in the central pit had burned down to glowing embers, and the occasional pop of crackling wood was the only sound that filled the space. The wide, circular tent felt larger in the quiet, its soft walls stretching upward toward the open sky, revealing glimpses of stars through the thin mesh of the roof's central opening.

Zivah stood, the quiet weight of the evening pressing gently upon her. With practiced grace, she moved through the tent to her adjacent sleeping quarters, more fitting for a young girl. The delicate bells attached to the hem of her robe jingled softly with each step. Her nightly routine was simple yet comforting and familiar. First, she undid the small silver clasp that held her braided hair in place, allowing the dark, heavy strands to fall freely down her back. She massaged her scalp lightly, her fingers working through the knots that had formed over the day.

Next, she crossed to the small copper basin near her sleeping mat, dipping her hands into the cool water and bringing it to her face. The sharp chill refreshed her, droplets tracing soft lines down her neck as she wiped them away with the towel draped over the basin. Her reflection in the small bronze mirror was faint in the dim light, but it was one she had known all her life. Tonight, though, something felt different. Her own eyes seemed distant as if some part of her was already slipping into a dream she hadn't yet begun.

She shook off the feeling, attributing it to the excitement of seeing Asher and the looming weight of their upcoming marriage in a few months. The weeks ahead would be filled with preparations, family gatherings, and endless advice from her elders. But tonight, she was alone in the stillness of her home, her mind beginning to drift toward sleep.

After removing her robe, Zivah slipped into her thin nightgown and knelt beside her sleeping mat. The familiar smell of sandalwood incense, lingering from her mother's evening prayers, mingled with the earthy scent of the woven rugs and woollen blankets that lined the tent. She lay back, her body sinking into the soft layers of fabric, the cool air from outside brushing lightly against her exposed skin.

The firelight flickered one last time before dimming into embers, casting long, distorted shadows against the curved walls of the tent. Zivah's gaze wandered toward the stars visible through the roof's opening, the night sky stretching out like an endless sea of darkness. Her thoughts drifted once more to Asher—his touch, his gentle voice, and the way he had looked at her tonight with such warmth. She smiled, letting her eyes close as her body relaxed into the familiar comfort of her bed.

But as sleep crept in, something shifted. Her mind began to pull away from the present, tugged by a force she didn't understand. The sensation was faint at first, like a distant whisper, but it grew stronger with each passing moment. It was as if the edges of her reality were blurring, dissolving into something else entirely.

The softness of the woollen blankets beneath her gave way to the sensation of cool, dewy earth. The scent of incense was replaced by something far more elusive—wildflowers, fresh rain, and something older, something she couldn't quite place. The air around her thickened, and when she opened her eyes, she was no longer inside her tent.

She was standing in a garden.

A strange, beautiful garden. For Zivah, this is when things became strange.

It began as a flicker—just a sliver of an image in her mind, something glimpsed out of the corner of her eye. A shadow, a presence, pulling her deeper into anticipation, teasing her like the start of a half-remembered memory.

She stood alone in the garden, but it was not just any garden. There was something unnatural about it. Statues of long-forgotten figures loomed around her, their stone faces turned toward her, watching. The air felt heavy, weighed down by a thick mist that clung to her skin. Tall hedges rose like walls around her, trapping her in the garden and cutting off any path to escape. The mist—it moved with a life of its own, curling around her legs, whispering through the leaves, as if it were guiding her deeper into this strange dream.

In the distance, she heard a soft giggle—childlike and teasing. She spun around, searching the fog, but there was nothing. Only shadows.

Her body responded, though—alive, tingling, anticipating something she couldn't yet name. She felt him before she saw him. His presence moved around her, playing with her, like a predator circling its prey. The air vibrated with his energy, a low hum that made her heart race. Zivah's breath quickened, her pulse hammering in her chest. She turned again, desperately trying to catch a glimpse of him. But all she saw was the mist, the statues, and the garden closing in.

Then she felt it—a touch on her right wrist. Barely there, ever so slight, but solid, like the trunk of a tree. Her breath caught in her throat. It wasn't a dream. It was real. Whoever, or whatever, was playing with her was as real as the earth beneath her feet.

She turned, her eyes wide, but again—nothing. The mist swirled, thick and impenetrable, hiding him from view.

Then came the voice, soft, intimate, brushing against her ear like a lover's breath. "Close your eyes... and open your mind." The words slipped into her like a command, their meaning wrapping around her senses, setting her body ablaze with a desire she had never known.

Zivah jolted awake, gasping. Her young body was on fire. Her skin tingled, flushed with heat, every inch of her alive with sensation. She could still feel him—the ghost of his touch on her wrist, the warmth of his breath against her neck. It was real. It had to be. No dream had ever left her body trembling like this, her mind spinning in a haze of confusion and want.

She lay there in the dim light of the tent, her pulse racing, her breath coming in shallow gasps. The pull was still there, inside her. Her body ached, craved something more—something she had never allowed herself to feel. She wanted him to come back. She wanted to be touched again.

What was happening to her? She had never felt anything like this before. Was this... normal? Or was this something darker? Something dangerous?

Slowly, she slipped out of bed, the cool night air brushing against her heated skin, but it did nothing to cool the fire that burned within her. Her movements were slow, deliberate, as if she were savouring every second of this strange, new feeling. She crossed the tent, her bare feet brushing the floor as she reached for a sip of water, but even that felt different now, as though every part of her body was heightened, attuned to something greater.

She let her nightclothes fall to the floor, the fabric slipping away until she stood naked, exposed. Her skin prickled, her nipples hardening in the cold air, but it wasn't the chill that made her tremble. It was the memory of him—the way his presence had filled the garden, the way her body had reacted to his touch, his voice. She wanted to feel it again. She needed to.

Returning to bed, Zivah lay back on the thin sheets, her body tingling with anticipation. She closed her eyes, willing herself back into the dream, back to him. Her right hand drifted to her lips, her fingers brushing against her mouth. Slowly, her tongue flicked out to taste her skin, the sensation sending a shiver down her spine.

Her other hand moved down her body, tracing the curve of her neck, her collarbone, her breast. Her nipples were already hard, her breath quickening as she gently squeezed her breast, teasing the nipples between her fingers. It was his touch she imagined, not hers—the warmth of his hands, the way his fingers had barely grazed her skin before disappearing.

Her hand continued its slow descent, sliding over her hips, her thighs, until she found the heat between her legs. She gasped softly, as she reached for her warm, wet, pulsating, and tight vagina, she slowly touched her outer lips, pinching them between her fingers. Ever so gently, she slid her fingers slightly in to get some of her wetness, moving her fingers up and down the length of her lips, rolling them between her fingers. Then, she moved her fingers up to her clitoris, ever so gently twisting around it, teasing it to come out and play.

Finding herself rolling it between her index finger and thumb, Zivah's right hand caressed her breast, squeezing it until the nipple slipped through her fingers. With each rolling motion of her clitoris with her left hand, she also twirled her right nipple, squeezing harder and harder while arching her back as she slipped into a euphoric state she'd never experienced before. The motion built—faster, harder, faster, and harder.

"Close your eyes..." she heard him say. Her fingers moved faster, her breath coming in short, ragged gasps. She was close—so close. Her body trembled, the tension building, coiling tighter and tighter inside her. She needed him back. She needed to feel him.

And then, suddenly, she was there again.

The garden. The mist. And him.

This time, he stood before her. The man—or was he a man? His form was tall, broad-shouldered, but his face was shrouded in shadow. His presence filled the space around them, overwhelming her senses. There was something otherworldly about him, something both beautiful and terrifying. His eyes glowed faintly in the mist, catching the light in strange ways, as though he weren't entirely human.

He moved toward her, his footsteps silent in the thick fog. His hand reached out, finding the back of her neck with a firm, possessive grip. She gasped, her knees going weak beneath her. His touch was hot, too hot—like fire seeping into her skin, making her shiver. But she wanted more. She needed more.

He leaned in close, his breath brushing against her lips, but he didn't kiss her. Not yet. He hovered there, teasing her with his nearness. She ached for him to touch her, to take her. The anticipation was unbearable.

"Close your eyes..." he whispered, his voice dark, seductive. "Melt into the moment."

She obeyed, her body surrendering completely. His hand tightened on her neck, pulling her closer as his lips found her skin—her neck, her collarbone, her breasts. His touch was fire, searing her skin, but she didn't care. She wanted to burn. She wanted to melt into him, to be consumed by him.

His hands roamed over her body, firm and sure, exploring every inch of her as though he owned her. His lips moved lower, teasing her breasts, his tongue flicking over her nipples, sending a jolt of pleasure through her. Her breath came faster, her body trembling beneath his touch.

She leaped onto him like a lioness claiming her prey, causing him to lose balance and fall backward onto the dewy grass. His garment slipped away, revealing the hard lines of his muscular body, and there, before her, stood his cock—erect, throbbing with veins that pulsed beneath the taut skin. Zivah's breath hitched, her heart hammering in her chest, unsure of what to do, yet overcome with the burning desire to taste him, to feel him in her mouth.

Without hesitation, she leaned down, her lips parted, and slowly took him into her mouth, her tongue swirling around the head of his circumcised cock. She felt him stiffen beneath her, heard the low growl of pleasure that escaped his throat, urging her on. Her hands slid up and down his chest, her fingers tracing the contours of his muscles as her mouth moved lower down his shaft.

Her lips squeezed tightly as she came back up, her mouth forming a perfect, warm tunnel around him. She bobbed up and down, her tongue dancing over his sensitive skin, savouring the taste of him. Each movement made him tremble beneath her, his moans filling the air, blending with the soft rustle of the mist around them.

Her body ached for more. Her swollen, wet pussy throbbed with need, craving to feel him inside her. She needed him now.

With deliberate slowness, Zivah slithered up his body, letting his now wet, dripping cock slide along her breasts, then her belly, until she was face-to-face with him once more. She kissed him deeply, passionately, her lips devouring his as though he were the only thing that could satisfy the growing hunger inside her. Her hands cradled his face, fingers digging into the firm skin of his jaw as she kissed him naughtily, eagerly, like a woman desperate to feel more.

Still holding his face with her right hand, she reached down with her left, gripping his rock-hard cock that now felt impossibly warm and full of promise. She slid the head along her slick lips, teasing herself, teasing him, coating him in her wetness. The sensation of his tip gliding against her sent a shiver up her spine. When she could wait no longer, she guided him inside, slowly lowering herself onto him, feeling the heat of him fill her completely.

She let out a soft gasp as he filled her, her hands moving to his chest to steady herself. Her hips began to rock gently, back and forth, slowly at first, as she adjusted to the sensation of his length inside her. Each movement sent shockwaves of pleasure through her body, igniting something deep inside. She could feel every inch of him, his cock rubbing against her sensitive walls as she began to move harder and faster, riding him with growing urgency.

He grabbed her hips, guiding her rhythm, his touch firm and commanding, allowing her to lose herself in the moment. She moved with him, her body swaying in ways she never knew possible. Her breasts bounced as she rode him, her nipples hard and aching with need. She leaned back, her fingers finding her clit, rubbing in tight circles as she felt the pleasure building inside her like a wave ready to crash.

His hands reached up to cup her breasts, his thumbs brushing over her nipples, flicking them with a rhythm that matched her movements. She gasped, her back arching as the sensation overwhelmed her. He leaned up, taking one of her nipples into his mouth, sucking, flicking, teasing it with his tongue while she ground her hips against him, desperate for release.

It was too much. The pleasure coiled tighter and tighter inside her, building with each thrust of his cock, each flick of his tongue. Her body trembled, the tension mounting until it became unbearable.

And then, she exploded.

Her orgasm ripped through her like a storm, her entire body quaking as wave after wave of pleasure crashed over her. She cried out, her nails digging into his chest as her body convulsed around him, her wet, tight pussy squeezing him in rhythmic pulses. The sensation sent him over the edge, and he flipped her over, his body still driving into hers.

Now on her stomach, her hips raised, she felt him thrust into her from behind, his cock filling her over and over again. He grabbed her hair, tugging gently, arching her back so that her breasts hung above the ground, her body fully exposed to him. He pounded into her, harder, faster, each thrust hitting her sweet spot, sending shockwaves through her already trembling form. She gasped, her breath hitching as his thumb slid into her tight, puckered anus, adding a new, dizzying sensation.

She could feel another orgasm building, more intense than the last, her body shaking with pleasure she had never thought possible. His cock thrust in and out, rubbing her G-spot as she reached back between her legs to rub her clit in time with his movements. The pressure built quickly, her mind spinning as she lost control.

"I'm going to come again!" she cried out, her voice strained with the intensity of the sensation. She was lost in the rhythm of their bodies, his cock thrusting deep into her, his thumb filling her ass, her fingers working her clit. The pleasure built higher and higher until she thought she might break.

And then it happened.

She let go completely, her body convulsing in an earth-shattering orgasm that left her gasping for air, her pussy clenching tightly around him, milking his cock as he pounded into her. She felt him shudder behind her, his cock swelling as he thrust deep inside one last time, his body shaking with the force of his release. He came with a grunt, filling her with his hot cum, his cock throbbing inside her as her own orgasm rocked through her again.

They collapsed together, their bodies tangled in a mass of slick skin and trembling limbs. Zivah lay face down, her heart racing, her breath coming in shallow gasps as the aftershocks of her orgasm continued to ripple through her. She could still feel him inside her, the warmth of his cum filling her, the memory of their connection burning like fire in her veins.

But when she opened her eyes, he was gone.

The tent was empty, the cool night air brushing against her sweat-dampened skin. She lay there, her body still trembling, her mind spinning in a haze of euphoria and confusion. The heat of him, the sensation of his touch, still lingered, but she was alone.

Had it all been a dream?

Her heart still raced, her skin still tingled, but she couldn't shake the feeling that something had changed. Whether real or not, it had been the most intense, glorious experience of her life. Her body ached for more, even as exhaustion began to settle in.

Zivah lay there, her mind drifting between the dream world and the waking world. The sensation of him still clung to her skin—the way he filled her completely, the way his presence had wrapped around her like a shadow. Her breath slowed, her muscles softening into the cool sheets, but something in the air still felt charged, as though the dream hadn't truly ended.

Then, in the corner of the tent, she saw it.

A shadow.

It moved, just for a moment, slipping out of the entrance of the tent. Her heart skipped a beat, her breath catching in her throat. Had he been real? Had he been here with her? The lingering warmth of his touch, the heat between her thighs, felt too vivid to be imagined.

She blinked, unsure of what she had seen. Her body was exhausted, her mind spinning, but the shadow... the shadow had been there. Had it been real? Or just another part of the dream? Something far older, far more powerful than she could comprehend seemed to hover just at the edges of her awareness.

Zivah lay there for what felt like hours, staring at the ceiling of the tent, her mind buzzing with questions she didn't know how to answer. Who was he? What had happened to her? Was this a dream or something more? There was a presence in that dream—something ancient, something divine, and it had touched her in ways she couldn't yet understand.

Her body felt warm, satisfied, but her soul stirred uneasily. The shadow that had slipped from the tent wasn't just a figment of her imagination—it had felt too deliberate, too real, like it was watching her, waiting for her.

The dream had awoken something deep within her, something primal, something sacred. She couldn't shake the feeling that it wasn't over, that this was only the beginning of something far greater, something far more powerful than she could yet grasp.

Chapter 4

Flavius & Caius

The door loomed before them, heavy and silent, its presence gnawing at the edges of Flavius' thoughts. Over the years monks have carved their names into the wood as a mark of existence. "I was here," said one with no context for who it was.

"I've been thinking," he muttered, casting a glance toward the dim, cold cell that lay just beyond them. "This guy's been here for so long... don't you wonder who he really is? I mean, I doubt anyone remembers anymore."

Caius shot him a sharp look, his voice low and dangerous. "Shut up, idiot. You don't want to be caught asking questions."

Flavius hesitated but pressed on, quieter this time. "But don't you wonder why they keep him locked away? All these years, and no one speaks of him." Flavius' voice dropped to a whisper, his stomach knotting as Caius' glare cut through the dim light.

"I said shut up," Caius hissed, cutting him off. "You know the rules," Caius snapped, his hand brushing the hilt of his blade. "Keep asking questions, and it won't just be the prisoner locked away." A faint scraping sound echoed from the cell, so soft it could have been imagined. Flavius stiffened, his eyes darting toward the door. Caius didn't flinch, but his jaw tightened, and his hand hovered near his weapon.

The corridor fell silent again, but this time, it wasn't natural. The air seemed to hum with a faint vibration, barely perceptible, like a breath held too long. Flavius glanced at Caius, but his companion's gaze was fixed on the door. For a moment, Caius' expression faltered, his confidence replaced by something Flavius hadn't seen before—*fear*.

Chapter 5

The Ritual Begins

"Joshua? Where are you?" Zivah's voice echoed through the small room, a hint of unease in her tone. She could have sworn she heard whispers.

Out from behind the old wooden bench, Joshua scrambled forward, his little hands dusty, eyes wide with mischief. "Here I am, Mumma!" His voice was bright, innocent—just like any five-year-old's. "Did you miss me?"

Zivah sighed in relief, smiling down at him though her heart still raced. "What were you doing back there?"

"Playing with my friend," Joshua said, glancing back toward the shadowed corner behind the bench. "He's really fun."

Zivah frowned. "Friend? Who's back there?" She stepped closer, peering into the shadows, but saw nothing.

Joshua beamed. "Just a friend, Mumma. He does cool tricks. He can make things disappear and come back again. Sometimes, he disappears too. He's really good at it."

Her smile faltered. "Really? Well... maybe your friend can join us for supper?"

Joshua turned and looked toward the shadows. "I'll go ask him." He ran back behind the bench, crouching low, whispering to someone just out of sight. Zivah took a step closer, heart thumping harder now.

The shadows seemed to move, to thicken. Joshua's small voice came again, "He says he can't come now. He's busy." Joshua paused, tilting his head as if listening to something only he could hear. Then he added in a whisper, "But he'll come back later."

Zivah's heart skipped. Her hand tightened on the back of the bench. "Joshua... Who are you talking to?"

Joshua stood up slowly, his face serious, the childish grin gone. "My friend. But you scared him away."

Zivah's breath caught. "What's his name?"

"I can't say it," Joshua said, a strange gleam in his eyes. "It's a secret name."

Her stomach twisted, but she forced a smile. "Oh... okay then. Come on, let's eat."

At the table, Joshua picked at his food, fidgeting in his seat, his eyes darting around the room as if waiting for something—or someone. Zivah watched him closely. He'd always been a picky eater, but tonight felt different.

"Eat your supper," Zivah said firmly, her voice cutting through the thick silence. "You need to eat everything to grow big and strong."

Joshua paused, his fork hovering over the food. "Like Malleck?" he asked suddenly, his tone shifting, a seriousness that felt far too old for a boy his age.

Zivah froze, the name unfamiliar and unsettling. "Malleck? Who's Malleck?"

Joshua chewed thoughtfully, his eyes distant as if remembering something from long ago. "You remember him, Mumma. He was the biggest of the ones who came to see me when I was born."

Zivah's heart pounded in her chest. "Joshua... what are you talking about?"

"You know. The ones that came when I was born," Joshua said casually, but his gaze was far too focused. "Malleck was there. He said he'd protect me."

Zivah blinked, her mouth dry. "Who... told you his name?"

Joshua smiled faintly. "I just know it. I remember everything."

That night, after putting Joshua to bed, Zivah lingered outside his room, unsettled. She could hear him talking softly, but the words were too quiet, too strange. Curiosity—or maybe fear—compelled her to peek through the crack in the doorway.

Her blood turned to ice.

There, sitting on the edge of Joshua's bed, were six beings. Shadows made flesh, their shapes flickering in and out of focus as if they were only half-real. Their eyes glowed faintly, focused entirely on Joshua. He didn't sound like himself anymore. His voice, usually light and innocent, now held a chilling authority.

"They accused you," Joshua said softly, addressing one of the beings, "but they were wrong. I will free you from the in-between."

Zivah's heart hammered in her chest. These weren't imaginary friends. They were real.

One of the beings, a tiny, fury figure barely four inches tall, spoke in a trembling voice. "How... how did I get stuck here?"

Joshua closed his eyes, his small face suddenly far too calm and wise. "You were careless," he said, his voice low, resonant. "You tried to steal from someone too powerful for you."

Zivah pressed her back against the wall, fear clawing at her. How did her son know these things? How could he remember things that had never been spoken of? Her mind raced, flashing back to the night of his birth, to the strange figures that had watched from the shadows.

Without warning, Joshua's head tilted slightly, his voice softening but never losing that strange authority. "Mum's watching us."

The beings turned in unison, their glowing eyes fixing on the crack in the door. Zivah's heart nearly stopped. She stepped back, her breath ragged, but before she could move the door creaked and slowly closed as if obeying an unseen command.

Zivah stumbled back from the door, her heart hammering against her ribs. The door had closed on its own—Joshua had made it close. But how?

She pressed her palms against her temples, trying to steady her breathing, to quiet the frantic thoughts racing through her mind. "This isn't real", she told herself. But the memory of his birth, the strange whispers, the shadows that moved when no one looked— everything she had brushed aside as her own paranoia now rushed back with terrifying clarity.

But the memory of those glowing eyes, fixed on her in eerie unison, was too vivid to be a dream.

For a moment, Zivah stood frozen in the hallway, her back pressed against the cold wall, trying to decide what to do. Should she go back in and confront whatever was happening? Or should she run? Call for help?

But help from whom? No one knew. No one could know about Joshua—about his birth, about the strange things he remembered. She had kept it secret all these years, brushing it off as childish imagination. But now... she wasn't so sure.

The air around her seemed heavier now, charged with something unnatural. She swallowed hard, gathering her courage, and crept quietly back toward the door. Maybe she'd imagined the whole thing. Maybe Joshua was just dreaming, talking in his sleep, and the rest was some trick of the light.

Zivah pressed her ear to the door again, holding her breath. Inside, Joshua's voice continued, but now it was softer, almost a whisper. The others—those shadowy beings—remained silent, but their presence was unmistakable. They were listening to him with rapt attention, like soldiers awaiting their command.

"We have to find the way back," Joshua was saying, his tone calm but authoritative. "The old paths are closed, but there are others. I know where to look."

One of the creatures, a figure tall and thin, its edges flickering like smoke, spoke in a low rasp. "The boy is too young. The power may consume him."

Joshua laughed softly. "I'm not too young. I've been here before."

Zivah's breath hitched in her throat. She couldn't understand what he meant—how could her son, barely five years old, be speaking like this? How could he have such knowledge? Such control?

What is happening?

"How will we find the paths, master?" a new voice asked. This one was deeper, more commanding, yet filled with reverence.

"Through the Great Hall of Memories," Joshua replied. "I can access it. I've already been there, and I'll return again."

Zivah's skin prickled. The Hall of Memories? The name itself stirred something deep within her, a faint recollection from stories she had long forgotten, stories whispered by her grandmother in hushed tones when Zivah had been a child herself.

The silence in the room thickened. Zivah dared to peer through the keyhole in the door, just for a moment.

The others were still there, their shadowy forms seated in a loose circle around the bed. Joshua was in the centre, his small body rigid, his face calm, serene, almost unnaturally so. He sat with his hands clasped in his lap, his eyes half-closed, as if in deep thought—or something far darker.

"We'll need the items for the ritual," Joshua said suddenly, his voice cutting through the stillness. "Water. Bread. A knife. And a chalice. I think Mumma has them in the kitchen."

Zivah's breath caught in her throat. A ritual?

"We can't do it now, master," one of the figures protested, its voice thin and whistling. "The time isn't right."

Joshua shook his head, his expression tightening. "I decide when the time is right. We do it now. He's waiting for us."

The others shifted uneasily, their glowing eyes flickering like embers in the dark.

"But Malleck—" the voice began again before being cut off by a sharp gesture from Joshua.

"Enough," Joshua snapped, his voice filled with an authority no child should possess. "I know what I'm doing."

Zivah's heart raced. She had to stop this. Whatever it was, whatever Joshua was planning, she couldn't let it happen. She wasn't sure what this "ritual" was or who this "Malleck" was, but the mere mention of his name sent a shiver down her spine.

She stepped back from the door, her mind racing. If she stormed in, if she confronted him... what would happen? Would Joshua even recognize her in this state? Or had something else taken over her son entirely?

Suddenly, the door creaked open on its own.

Zivah gasped, stumbling backwards as Joshua stood in the doorway, his eyes wide, innocent. He smiled up at her as though nothing strange had happened at all.

"Mumma?" he asked softly. "Why are you out here?"

Zivah's mouth went dry. She stared at him, unable to find her voice. He looked so... normal. His face, round and soft, full of the boyish charm she was used to. But behind his eyes, there was something else. Something watching her. Waiting.

"I—I heard you talking," she stammered, her voice trembling. "Who were you talking to, Joshua?"

Joshua's smile widened, but there was something unsettling in it now. A coldness behind the sweetness. "Just my friends, Mumma. They had to go. But they'll be back."

Zivah swallowed hard, trying to keep her composure. "What... what were you talking about?"

Joshua's eyes flickered. He tilted his head, almost as if weighing whether or not to tell her the truth. Then he smiled again, that same innocent, eerie smile.

"Just stories, Mumma. Just stories."

Later that night, after Zivah had finally convinced herself to leave Joshua alone and return to her room, the house fell into an eerie quiet. The kind of silence that felt unnatural, like the world itself was holding its breath.

Joshua lay in his bed, wide awake, staring at the ceiling. The shadows in the corners of the room twisted and writhed, alive with the presence of the others. But now, they were quiet, waiting.

He turned his head slightly as if listening to something far away. Then he whispered, "It's time."

The shadows stirred, and one by one, the others appeared again, flickering into being, their forms half-real, half-illusion. They gathered around Joshua, their glowing eyes fixed on him with reverence.

"Master," one of them rasped, its voice low and reverent. "Is the time truly now?"

Joshua nodded, his face serene. "Yes. We will bring him back."

He slid out of bed, moving with a grace far beyond his years, and crept silently down the hall to the kitchen. The others followed him, their forms barely making a sound as they glided through the darkness.

In the kitchen, Joshua gathered the items he needed: a chalice, a loaf of bread, and a small knife. His tiny hands worked quickly, efficiently, as though he had done this a thousand times before. The others watched in silence, their eyes glowing softly in the dim light.

While he's there, he notices a strange presence, another being, tall, in black cloth and floating while hiding in the dark corner of the room just off the kitchen. Joshua pretends not to have seen him and observes what it does while he is collecting everything he needs. This mysterious being just grins and moves further back into the shadow until it's gone and the only thing left was a small mist dissipating and a smell so delicious his mouth waters just thinking about it. Joshua knows this being, the elusive creature that it is. It prefers people to think it doesn't exist. That's how it can manipulate humans to do what it wants, and they have no idea why they do them. They just do. It takes great joy in this game. Joshua knows this game too, and somehow the creature knows he knows it. Joshua gets the feeling he'll be back.

As he returned to his room, Joshua paused for a moment, his gaze drifting toward his mother's room. Zivah was asleep, her chest rising and falling gently, her face peaceful.

Joshua smiled faintly, but it was not a smile of love or warmth. It was a smile of understanding—a smile of someone who knew far more than he should.

Joshua placed the chalice and loaf of bread on the floor in the centre of his room, arranging the items with careful precision. The others, those strange, half-shadow beings, formed a circle around him, their eyes gleaming in the darkness like dim embers.

The air was heavy, thick with the weight of something unseen, something ancient.

Joshua took a deep breath, closing his eyes, and the others followed suit, their forms flickering, their bodies barely solid in the dim light. Their presence felt oppressive, as though the space they occupied was bending under the strain of forces that didn't belong in this world.

He opened his eyes slowly, his face expressionless, his hands steady as he lifted the small knife. "Hic est sanguis meus novi testamenti, qui pro multis effundetur in remissionem peccatorum." His voice was calm, reverent, as if he'd spoken these words countless times. "This is my blood of the new covenant, which is shed for the many for the release of sins."

With a deliberate movement, Joshua sliced the tip of his finger, letting the blood drip into the chalice. As each drop fell, the water inside darkened, turning red like wine—or something far more ancient and primal.

The others shifted slightly, murmuring in low voices, their words incomprehensible, their shapes vibrating with a strange energy. They watched Joshua closely, their loyalty unquestioning, their eyes never leaving him.

Joshua placed the knife down carefully and picked up the loaf of bread. He held it out before him, his small hands steady, his face calm and focused. "Hoc est corpus meum, quod pro vobis tradetur. Hoc facite in meam commemorationem." His voice, though soft, carried an undeniable authority. "This is my body, which is given for you. Do this in remembrance of me."

He tore the bread in two, placing it on the floor beside the chalice. The room grew colder, the temperature plummeting as though a door to another world had been opened, allowing something dark and ancient to creep through.

The shadows in the corners of the room deepened, swirling like smoke, thickening with every word Joshua spoke. He closed his eyes again, taking a deep breath, as if drawing in the very essence of the air around him.

"Surge, Malleck, et dimittam te de servitute tua, ut consurgas ante me." Joshua's voice was low, a whisper that seemed to resonate far beyond the walls of the room. "Rise, Malleck, I release you from your bondage. I command you to rise before me."

The others leaned in closer, their eyes glowing more intensely, their forms rippling as though they were being pulled toward something unseen. They repeated the words with him, their voices blending into a haunting chorus. "Surge, Malleck, et dimittam te de servitute tua, ut consurgas ante me."

The room seemed to shudder, the very air vibrating with the weight of the incantation. The symbols Joshua had drawn on the floor began to glow faintly, pulsing with a sickly light. The blood in the chalice rippled as though something inside it was waking.

"Surge, Malleck, et dimittam te de servitute tua, ut consurgas ante me," Joshua repeated, his voice growing stronger, more insistent. The others joined in, their chant merging into a haunting hum that filled the room, vibrating with unnatural energy.

Outside the door, Zivah stood in the hallway, her heart pounding in her chest. She had heard Joshua leave his room earlier, moving silently through the house, but she hadn't followed. Something inside her had told her not to—something primal, some instinct that warned her not to witness what her son was doing.

But now, as she stood outside his door, she could feel the air around her shift, growing colder and heavier. She pressed her hand against the doorframe, unsure whether to push the door open or run the other way.

The silence was deafening. Then she heard Joshua's voice again, clear, commanding, far too powerful for a child of his age.

"Surge, Malleck, et dimittam te de servitute tua, ut consurgas ante me."

The floor beneath her feet seemed to vibrate as though the very earth was responding to the words. Zivah swallowed hard, her throat dry, and leaned closer to the door. She couldn't see anything, but she could feel it—something was happening inside that room. Something terrible.

Inside the room, Joshua's face was set with determination, his eyes locked on the chalice and the bread before him. The others were still, waiting, their bodies barely visible in the dim light. The air itself seemed to bend and warp, a strange distortion that made the walls seem closer, the shadows darker.

Joshua raised his hands over the chalice. "Surge, Malleck…" His voice faltered just for a second, a flicker of hesitation crossing his face. The others stirred, their eyes narrowing.

He clenched his fists, his resolve hardening. "I command you… to rise."

Suddenly, the shadows around the room swirled violently as though some unseen force had been unleashed. The symbols on the floor flared bright, casting a sickly red glow that filled the room. The chalice shook violently, the blood inside rippling, trembling, as though something within it was trying to break free.

The others stepped back, their forms blurring as the energy in the room intensified. Joshua remained still, his eyes locked on the glowing symbols. "Come forward, Malleck," he whispered, his voice barely audible over the growing hum of energy. "I free you from your chains. Rise… rise and serve me."

The air in the room grew thick, oppressive, as though all the oxygen had been sucked out. The others began to murmur, their voices low, uncertain.

Suddenly, a loud crack echoed through the room, like thunder striking the ground. The chalice shattered, spilling the blood-red liquid across the glowing symbols. The shadows recoiled violently, swirling faster and faster around the room before vanishing entirely, leaving only a thick, unnatural silence in their wake.

Joshua stood frozen, staring at the broken chalice, his face expressionless. The others looked at one another, unsure of what had just happened. They had expected something—someone—to rise from the in-between. But the room was empty, save for the shattered remnants of the ritual.

Zivah, still standing outside the door, heard the silence fall like a heavy weight. She felt a deep, cold fear settle in her bones, a knowing that whatever had just happened wasn't over. Something had changed, something had shifted, but she didn't understand what.

Inside, Joshua finally exhaled, his breath slow and measured. He knelt, dipping his finger into the spilled blood, tracing a single symbol onto the floor. The others watched him closely, their eyes still glowing faintly in the dark.

"It didn't work - did it?" one of them murmured, his voice tinged with disappointment.

Joshua looked up slowly, his eyes gleaming with something unreadable. "Not yet," Joshua said, a faint smile curling his lips as he traced another symbol on the floor with his blood. His voice softened, almost reverent. "But he's listening now, and when he comes, the veil will thin," Joshua murmured, his gaze fixed on the blood-soaked symbols. "And they'll all see what lies beyond the veil," Joshua murmured, his gaze unwavering. "What was hidden will be revealed, and no one will be able to look away."

Chapter 6

Caius & Flavius

"Oi, priest, wake up!" Flavius's voice cut through the stillness, sharp and urgent, like a blade slipping through the cold night air.

The small chamber beneath the Vatican was cold, lit only by dim, flickering candlelight. Stone walls, heavy with the weight of history, pressed in from all sides. The air was thick with the smell of incense and damp stone. Somewhere, deep in the hidden corridors, something shifted.

"Leave him," Caius muttered darkly, his words laced with a hint of mockery. "Let him dream. He's no doubt somewhere better than this place."

Flavius crouched near the slumped figure of a priest, who had fallen into an unnaturally deep sleep, a leather-bound book lying open on his lap. His hand instinctively hovered near his side, where a silvered cross dangled alongside a dagger, both more symbols of duty than faith.

"We're not here for dreams, Caius," Flavius hissed. "This isn't a game. it's stirring again."

A long silence passed between them, broken only by the faint sound of breathing from the corner of the room. Caius leaned against the stone wall, his eyes shadowed by the hood of his black robe. He crossed his arms, indifferent, his lips curving into a sneer.

"Stirring," he echoed, his voice dripping with disdain. "it's been stirring for a thousand years, and nothing has ever come of it."

Flavius turned his gaze toward the back of the chamber, where the shadows seemed to ripple like water. The figure behind the iron door was not visible, but Flavius could feel his presence, heavy and undeniable, like gravity itself.

"You don't know that," Flavius whispered, the weight of doubt settling in his chest. "You've heard the stories. They say he—"

"I don't care about stories," Caius snapped, cutting him off. "We do our job. We guard the room, we obey the Order, and we don't ask questions."

"Yeah..." Flavius muttered, his eyes still fixed on the darkened corners of the room. "But what if we're wrong? What if he's not dangerous? What if he's something else entirely?"

Caius' sneer widened. "Wrong about what? That he's dangerous? He's barely alive. The priests pump him so full of drugs he's more dead than alive."

"Then why guard him at all?" Flavius countered, his voice trembling with the questions he'd never dared to ask aloud before. "Why keep him locked away? Why the secrecy? What if—"

"Enough," Caius growled, pushing off the wall. "Stop letting the darkness get to your head, Flavius. This is your first rotation, I get it. The silence does things to you, makes you think strange thoughts. But nothing's going to change. He's been down here longer than anyone's been alive. This is our duty. You keep your mouth shut, you keep your head down, and you don't question the Order. Ever."

Flavius's grip tightened on his blade, his knuckles white under the dim light. He'd been trained to follow orders without hesitation, raised in the solitude of the monastery, never knowing the outside world. But in this cold, damp chamber, something had changed. Something had shifted.

There was a pull in the air, a vibration that thrummed in his bones, like an ancient memory trying to claw its way to the surface. Flavius stared at the sleeping priest, his whispers from earlier ringing in his ears: fragments of forgotten names, warnings half-spoken. The priest seemed so certain, his voice shaking with something between fear and awe. What did he know that Flavius didn't?

Flavius's gaze flickered back to the iron bars at the back of the chamber. In the depths of the shadows, the figure stirred again, not a movement of the body but of something deeper—an energy, a pulse that seemed to ripple through the air, brushing against Flavius's skin like a cold breath. He had never dared to look too closely before, but now... now he felt something he hadn't felt before.

A connection. A presence. Something not right.

For a brief moment, Flavius could almost hear a voice, distant and fractured, echoing through the corridors of his mind. It was not his own.

Help me!

"Flavius," Caius's voice cut through the strange haze. "Stay focused."

The moment passed, and Flavius blinked, the strange sensation fading as quickly as it had come. He stood up, shaking off the growing unease, but the question still lingered, like a bad smell near the chamber pots... gnawing at him.

What if the threat they were guarding wasn't a threat at all? What if they weren't guarding a monster? What if they were guarding salvation? And what if the Church's greatest fear wasn't losing control—but being exposed to the truth?

Chapter 7

Pawns in Time

"She's dying! We gotta do sumfing!" one of the creatures shouted, panic clear in its voice. The crowd shifted, a mass of nervous energy, their grotesque forms flickering in the fog.

"There's nothing we can do," another voice muttered, resigned, hollow.

"There has to be!" came a frantic response. "She can't die—he'll die!"

Chaos swirled through the fog as the creatures pressed in, desperate, helpless. Then, from the back of the crowd, a deep, steady voice broke through the cacophony.

"I know a way."

All eyes turned, the murmur of the crowd falling into silence. The figure who spoke was enormous—Malleck, a giant whose presence alone seemed to absorb the shadows. His towering silhouette absorbed the dim light, muscles rippling beneath dark, rough skin, exuding a strength that could break a man with ease. His broad shoulders and the sharp angles of his face gave him the look of a titan who had clawed his way from the depths of the earth, a being forged in a time when creatures of his size ruled without mercy.

Malleck projected a menacing persona—a carefully crafted mask of intimidation—it was, at its core, a fragile shield, a performance born from self-preservation. But if you looked beyond that exterior husk, there was something about him that tempered any fear—a gentle restraint in his movements, a perfected stilness. His massive hands, capable of crushing souls, were always steady and careful. His eyes, oversized, dark, and intense, carried the weight of a thousand years of sorrow and compassion. Beneath the terrifying exterior, he harboured something deeper: something more meaningful, reluctance even, a kindness he could not easily mask but tried to hide.

As Malleck tentatively stepped forward, his heavy, deliberate movements made the ground tremble beneath his feet. It was not long before he started to realise the weight of the choice he was about to make. This child was no ordinary child—Malleck knew that much. His birth had summoned powers from beyond the realms of men. His existence meant something far greater than any one life. Saving him meant hope for a world on the edge of collapse.

"Quick!" one of the others barked, tension rising again. "Whatever it is, just do it! We ain't got time!"

Malleck didn't move right away, his gaze locked on the frail form of Zivah lying on the ground. His hulking presence alone could make even the bravest of warriors shrink back, but there was hesitation in his eyes. He knew the cost. His voice, though steady, trembled slightly. "If I do this... I'm dead. If I do, I won't be coming back."

He hesitated for the briefest of moments. Did he fear death? No. What Malleck feared was the unknown—this oblivion that waited for him. Questions spun in his head like a spider getting ready for a night of feasting. Would he cease to exist? Would his memories, his essence, simply fade into the void? Or worse, would he linger somewhere, trapped between worlds, with nothing but the regret of what he gave up?

"Trust me, Malleck," a voice growled from the crowd, its edge sharp with desperation. "We're all dead if you don't."

Malleck slowly nodded before stepping forward through the fog, his immense frame parting the sea of creatures like a force of nature. As terrifying as he appeared, none dared challenge him. He stood over Zivah now, his shadow engulfing her fragile body, and the others watched in nervous anticipation, their eyes gleaming in the dim light.

His thick fingers hovered just inches above her, his enormous hands capable of both destruction and salvation. He paused, looking around at the gathered creatures for reassurance, but they gave none. They simply stared, waiting for him to act. One of the beasts behind him gave him a shove, urging him forward.

Malleck wasn't bothered. His massive shoulders rolled back as he took a deep breath. Closing his eyes, he bent low over Zivah's body, his large hands trembling slightly above her. Slowly, he opened his eyes again, locking his gaze deep into her, piercing through her flesh, searching for the tiny spark that kept her connected to life.

For a moment, nothing happened.

"Malleck!" a voice hissed from behind. "Hurry!"

Ignoring them, Malleck exhaled, his breath steady, powerful. Then, in a gentle whisper that seemed to carry the weight of eons, he uttered the ancient words that had been buried deep within him, even Malleck didn't know he knew them until now. The command, spoken in a language older than time, flowed from him like a sweet prayer.

The words slipped into the air, wrapping themselves around Zivah like a cocoon. Her body stiffened briefly before relaxing, her eyes fluttering closed as she fell into a deep, otherworldly sleep.

In the sky above, a thin, silk-like lightning bolt appeared, twisting and winding its way down through the dark clouds. The creatures gasped as it descended, slow and deliberate, before finally piercing Zivah's body. The light penetrated deep into her soul, intertwining with the very essence of her delicate being.

The other creatures, wide-eyed, whispered among themselves. Some cowered in fear of what they just witnessed, clutching at the fog as if it might swallow them whole. Others stared in awe, too afraid to move or speak.

As the last of Malleck's breath evaded him, his enormous form began to dissolve. The creatures watched in stunned silence as Malleck's body shimmered, dissolving into mist. He gave no cry of pain, no final words—he simply vanished into the fog, his essence scattered by the wind.

Did it work?
I think so.
We'll soon find out.

Malleck felt himself pulled from the world, sucked through an endless, twisting void. The stars above blurred, streaking past him like lines of light. Faster and faster he moved, drawn away from the place where he had stood, the place where he had lived. His body felt cold, the sensation of his own form slipping away—becoming something less than tangible. He could almost feel his memories unravelling, like threads fraying from a garment.

For a moment, he saw the entirety of creation stretched out before him—a vast, incomprehensible tapestry. Then, just as quickly, a blink even, it all slipped away, becoming no more than a faint memory like trying to hold onto a dream.

Who am I now? Am I still me? or am I now just part of nothingness? The thoughts lingered in his mind like an echo. Would his identity, too, be stripped away? Was he merely a collection of memories now, soon to be lost in this expanse of nothingness?

Everything started to slow down. The pull stopped, and Malleck found himself drifting in a strange, dreamlike place. He was surrounded by a faint glow of distant colours—soft, blurred, like memories that refused to take form. The stars around him flickered, hazy and indistinct, as though viewed from behind an opaque dome.

The weightlessness felt disorienting. He felt no ground beneath him, no sensation of being anchored to anything solid. He was alone. His own existence felt tenuous, as though he could drift apart at any moment. There was a strange coldness, not like the chill of air but a deeper, more hollow cold—a coldness of the soul.

"Am I dead?" Malleck muttered to himself, his voice echoing through the space around him. He moved his arms, testing the limits of his form, but found no resistance. "No... I can't be dead. I can still... think."

He floated there, lost in the haze of the stars, time slipping away. It could have been minutes, hours, or years—he couldn't tell. Then, from every direction at once, a voice spoke.

"You are in the nothingness... what you once called it," the voice said, cold and distant. "We call it Dark Matter."

Malleck shuddered. "Dark Matter?"

The voice continued, its tone sinister and calm, coming from all around him. "You are far removed from your old life, so distant in time that all who once knew you have forgotten.

You see things hazy because you are now inside the Dark Matter, looking out at the material world."

Malleck swallowed hard, his throat tight. The voice's words carried a weight that seemed to press against his very existence. Forgotten? He was one of them once—a protector, a presence. But now, the idea that time itself had erased him sent an icy chill through him.

"Can I go back?"

"No," the voice responded, flat and absolute. "You have no power to take yourself back."

"Am I dead, then?" Malleck's voice wavered, uncertainty gnawing at him. Is this it? Is this all that's left for me?

"You might as well be," the voice said with a hint of dark amusement. "But no, you are in what the humans once called purgatory. An in-between place. A place where those who use the old gods' wisdom are sent. This is the price you pay. A special kind of prison. Not good, not evil. It just... is."

Malleck closed his eyes, the weight of the words settling over him like a shroud. Why did I do this? Was it worth it? He had saved a life, but now he was in a place where time and memory meant nothing. "But I didn't abuse the power. I used it to save a life. Did it work? Did they survive?"

"Yes," the voice replied. "The woman and her child were saved. But the child... the child is not so simple."

Malleck's eyes snapped open, a knot forming in his chest. "What do you mean?"

There was a pause, and then the voice sighed as if recalling an ancient memory. "I remember... I remember the child's birth. But it's not as clear as it should be. I know the child you speak of. The child who was destined to know the old gods, to walk their paths. But his future is... strange."

Malleck frowned. "Strange how?"

"The child was supposed to be a bridge," the voice continued, its tone thoughtful now. "A bridge between the forgotten wisdom of the past and the chaos of the future. I was there. I was one of the Memory Keepers."

Malleck's breath caught. "A... Memory Keeper?"

"Yes," the voice whispered, and Malleck could feel a chill creep down his spine. "I held the memories of every being that ever lived, from the smallest insect to the greatest kings. I knew their fears, their desires, their triumphs, and their failures. I could see everything—the past, the present, and all the possible futures. But there was a price."

Malleck felt the weight of those words. A price? He understood sacrifice, but this?

"Knowledge is a curse, Malleck. When you know everything, you become detached from the world. You see all outcomes, all possibilities, but you cannot act. You cannot interfere. And eventually... you forget what it is to live. I... I grew tired. I longed to feel again. So I interfered, just once, in the life of a human. A priest."

"What happened?" Malleck asked, his voice barely a whisper.

"The priest was... insignificant. A man lost in his doubts, teetering between faith and reason. I whispered to him, guided him, showed him things beyond mortal comprehension. But that act—one simple whisper—broke the rules.

The other Memory Keepers punished me. They took away my sight of the future. Now, I see only the past... and the now. I am trapped in this Dark Matter, just like you."

Malleck floated in stunned silence, the vastness of the void pressing in on him.

"You see," the voice continued, "I once knew the child's fate. But now... it is hidden from me. I see fragments, broken pieces of what could have been. I remember him teaching love, peace, and unity. But there are multiple endings for his life, Malleck. And the most powerful one—the one that mattered—at least the one I think is the most important has been hidden."

Malleck's eyes narrowed as the voice continued.

"I can remember him dying," the voice said, each word dripping with dread. "He was tortured and killed. Brutally. Publicly. I see the crowds chanting on, I see the blood, I see the murder in their eyes, but then—" The voice faltered for a moment as if struggling to process its own recollection.

"Then what?" Malleck pressed, his voice rising in urgency.

"I see him rise back to life," the voice whispered. "I see him living again, only to disappear days later, fading into the shadows. There's another version of his death—where he fled, hid from the world, becoming a hermit in a distant land. But the final memory—it's blocked. There's nothing. Nothing in the sense that it's not even written."

"Blocked?" Malleck's voice was tight with confusion and frustration. "Who could block it?"

"I don't know," the voice muttered, its tone slipping into something close to fear. "From what I can tell, someone—or something—has erased the true outcome of the child. I can only see glimpses, fragments, but nothing more."

It's like I am trying to explain a dream, details slip past unnoticed.

"So he might still be alive," Malleck said, grasping for hope.

"Or he might be dead," the voice replied coldly. "My memory, like everything else in the universe, seems to be manipulated by someone. It is as though reality itself has been rewritten. Maybe... maybe he's alive."

Malleck stared out at the swirling colours of the void. "Could it be that his life was so unremarkable, so far removed from his destiny, that even you can't hold onto it? That's why the memory feels lost?"

The voice exhaled sharply, the irritation clear. "Poor memory?" it snapped mockingly. "You dare suggest that I could forget? That my grasp is so weak?"

"No, I didn't mean it that way," Malleck quickly replied. "I mean... the memory lost. Something taken. Could someone—something—erase it?"

There was a long pause. Finally, with reluctance, the voice spoke again. "If someone erased it, I would remember the act. The removal itself would be part of my records. But..."

The voice hesitated as though unwilling to concede.

Malleck pressed further. "But maybe... maybe there is something more powerful. Something even beyond the old gods."

A heavy silence followed, and for a moment, Malleck thought the voice wouldn't answer. Then, low and resigned, the voice whispered, "Yes... there are forces. Ancient. Older than even the gods we served. Forces that shape existence itself. They do not answer to us. Perhaps one of them found it... necessary to intervene."

"Necessary?" Malleck repeated, a cold realisation creeping over him. "Necessary for what?"

The voice chuckled darkly, though there was no amusement in the sound. "Perhaps you and I are just pawns in a game far greater than we understand."

Malleck floated in stunned silence, the vastness of the void pressing in on him. His mind spun with questions, with doubts, with the nagging feeling that he was closer to the truth than ever before... and yet still hopelessly far from it.

"A game?" Malleck finally muttered, his voice low, disbelieving. "What game?"

"The only one that matters," the voice whispered as if sharing a secret long buried beneath the weight of ages. "The game of power. Of control. You think you've made a sacrifice, Malleck? You think your death was noble? That you acted on your own free will?"

Malleck's chest tightened. "I acted to save a life. I acted because there was no other choice."

"Ah... and therein lies the trap," the voice replied, its tone filled with grim satisfaction. "No other choice. No other path. You see, Malleck, the game is not played by us. We are moved. Placed. Sacrificed as necessary."

Malleck clenched his fists, feeling the cold emptiness of the void tighten around him. "Moved by who?"

"By those who have always been in control," the voice hissed. "Those who pull the strings behind every decision, every fate. Greater than the old gods, greater than any being you've ever known. We serve them without knowing it, without ever questioning it."

"I don't serve anyone," Malleck growled, anger rising in his chest, a fire in the cold emptiness. "I chose to save the child. That was my decision."

"Your decision?" The voice laughed, this time with genuine amusement, but the sound was hollow, cruel. "Do you truly believe that? You played your part, Malleck. Just as I did when I whispered to the priest. Just as we all do. We are guided, our actions dictated, shaped. And we... we believe it is our will."

Malleck's mind reeled. Could it be true? Had he been nothing more than a piece on a larger board, a pawn in a game he couldn't even see?

"What... what is this game?" Malleck demanded, his voice harsher, more desperate now. "Who controls it?"

"Not gods. Not mortals. Not beings bound by flesh or spirit. But forces—forces older than the universe itself. They whisper in the silence, shift the tides of fate. They use the old gods as puppets, just as the gods use mortals. And we..." The voice trailed off, a hint of weariness seeping into its once-condescending tone.

"Pawns." Malleck finished the thought, his voice hollow. "You said we are pawns."

"Yes. Pawns. And pawns are the first to be sacrificed when the stakes rise."

Malleck's thoughts raced, the weight of the voice's words pressing down on him like a vice. The child... had it all been part of some larger design? Was his sacrifice meaningless, orchestrated from the start? And if so, for what purpose?

He struggled to maintain his composure, but doubt gnawed at him. "If we are pawns, what is the endgame? What do they want?"

The voice was silent for a long moment as if considering whether to reveal a truth too terrible to speak. When it finally answered, the voice was quieter, almost resigned. "The endgame? The endgame is always the same, Malleck. It's not about winning. It's about... balance."

"Balance?" Malleck echoed, his brow furrowed. "Balance between what?"

"Between creation and destruction. Between existence and oblivion. It's a cycle—one that repeats over and over. Universes are born, they die, and in the in-between, there is chaos. The forces that control us—they don't want the chaos. They seek to maintain the balance, to prevent the cycle from being disrupted."

"And the child?" Malleck's voice sharpened, a knot of fear twisting in his chest. "What role does he play in all this?" Is he meant to keep this going? Or destroy it?.

The voice sighed, a sound that echoed through the emptiness like a distant storm. "That is the question, isn't it? That is what even they—the ones who control the game—cannot fully see. The child... he is the anomaly. He is the piece that doesn't fit. He could tip the balance, either toward creation... or toward destruction."

Malleck's heart pounded in his chest, the gravity of the revelation sinking in. "Then my sacrifice... it was for nothing."

"No," the voice whispered, its tone growing darker, heavier. "Your sacrifice was necessary. To keep the child alive. To keep the game in motion. But what happens next... is beyond your control. You need to come to terms with that."

Malleck's mind swirled with fear and uncertainty. If the child was the key to tipping the balance, then everything he had done, every life he had touched, was part of something far more dangerous than he could have ever imagined.

"What happens next?" Malleck demanded, desperation seeping into his voice. "Tell me."

The voice paused again as if savouring the moment. Then, with a cold finality, it answered, "What happens next... depends on the others."

Malleck's breath caught in his throat. "Others?"

"Yes," the voice whispered, the darkness around them seeming to tighten. "Others like you. Pawns. Pieces placed on the board. Some of them know the child... and some will stop at nothing to ensure he never fulfils his role."

Malleck's chest tightened. "Who are they? Where are they?"

"They are everywhere," the voice replied, its tone shifting as if it were fading into the vastness of the void. "And they are watching. Even now."

A cold chill ran down Malleck's spine as he realised the full weight of the situation. Forces were in motion—forces he couldn't begin to understand. And worse, the game was far from over.

"But who... who do I fight?" Malleck's voice cracked, panic edging into his words.

The voice, now barely more than a whisper in the dark, replied, "The question isn't who you fight, Malleck... it's whether you can trust anyone at all."

Before Malleck could respond, a sudden pulse of energy ripped through the void, and the voice fell silent, swallowed by the darkness. Malleck now alone, drifting, his mind racing with questions—questions he feared he might never get the answers to.

And in that moment, he understood—to him, the real game had only just begun.

Chapter 8

Flavius & Caius

The torches burned low, sputtering softly as seconds dragged into minutes, which dragged into hours. Each flicker of the flame cast jagged shadows that danced along the cold stone walls, twisting into shapes that seemed alive. Flavius shifted uneasily, his weight moving from one foot to the other, trying to shake the deep chill that had seeped into his bones. A steady drip echoed somewhere above in the chamber dome—a haunting rhythm that only deepened the oppressive silence.

Caius sat slouched against the wall, his back turned to the iron door they were tasked with guarding. His posture was deceptively relaxed, knees bent, arms draped loosely over them. His half-closed eyes betrayed nothing, but Flavius could see the tension in the subtle twitch of his jaw, the way his fingers flexed every so often.

The silence gnawed at Flavius. It wasn't just the quiet of an empty corridor; it was heavier, almost sentient. The shadows around them didn't merely shift—they seemed to pulse as though they were breathing. He cleared his throat, trying to dispel the weight in his chest.

"How much longer?" he muttered, his voice cracking. He hadn't meant to sound so nervous. It was supposed to be a routine shift, but nothing about this night felt routine.

Caius didn't respond at first, his eyes fixed on a point in the darkness. Then, with a slow exhale, he said, "Until we're relieved. Just like always." His tone was clipped, irritated. "What did you expect? A miracle?"

Flavius glanced at the iron door, its surface covered in a faint layer of frost. Beyond it lay the prisoner—a being cloaked in shadow and legend. "It's different tonight," he said, hesitating. "Don't you feel it?"

Caius's eyes snapped fully open, pinning Flavius in place. "Feel what?" His voice was sharp, but Flavius caught the edge of something beneath it—fear. "You're letting this place get to you. Don't start."

"I'm not imagining it," Flavius said, more firmly this time. He gestured toward the door, though his hand trembled slightly. "There's... movement. And I swear I heard whispers."

Caius froze, his knuckles tightening on his knees. His expression hardened, but the flicker of fear was unmistakable now. "Do not speak of the whispers," he hissed. His voice dropped to a near growl. "First whispers, then screams. And when you hear the screams, they drag you away—no explanations. You don't come back."

Flavius's stomach knotted. "But if there's—"

"No!" Caius snapped, cutting him off. He straightened, his voice sharp as a blade. "You're not the first to hear them, Flavius. It's this place. It gets inside your head. Just do your duty, and keep your mouth shut."

The iron door rattled.

Both men froze. The sound wasn't loud, but in the heavy silence, it was deafening. Flavius's heart slammed against his ribs as the metal groaned, the hinges straining under some unseen pressure. His hand flew to the hilt of his blade, though it felt useless in the face of whatever might be beyond that door.

"Did you hear that?" Flavius whispered, his voice barely audible.

Caius didn't answer immediately. His eyes were locked on the door, his body unnaturally still. Then, with forced calm, he muttered, "It's just the hinges. Old iron. It... shifts."

The door rattled again, followed by a soft, rhythmic scratching. Flavius's breath hitched. The sound was faint but unmistakable, like nails dragging across stone. It sent a shiver down his spine.

"Caius," Flavius said, his voice trembling. "What if—"

"Don't," Caius growled, cutting him off again. He stood, his movements stiff, deliberate. "Don't go near it."

Flavius took a half step forward, his instincts warring with his fear. "But what if—"

"I said no!" Caius's hand shot out, gripping Flavius' arm like a vice. His eyes, usually cold and unreadable, now they were wide with something Flavius hadn't seen before: panic.

The scratching stopped.

For a moment, the silence was even worse. The air felt heavier, pressing down on them like a burden. Flavius opened his mouth to speak, but no sound came out. His heart pounded, each beat echoing in his ears.

Then came the voice.

"Help... me."

It wasn't a whisper, nor a scream. It was a plea—soft, broken, and filled with desperation. It came from beyond the iron door, but it felt as though it wrapped around Flavius, seeping into his very soul.

Flavius staggered back, his blade slipping slightly in his trembling grip. "Did you hear that?" he asked, his voice barely more than a breath.

Caius's face was pale, his lips pressed into a tight line. He didn't answer. Instead, he yanked Flavius back, shoving him against the wall. His grip was iron, his voice low and furious. "You didn't hear anything. Do you understand me? You didn't hear it."

"But—" Flavius started, but Caius's grip tightened, cutting him off.

"Do. You. Understand?" Caius's eyes burned with urgency, his voice trembling now. "You heard nothing. You say nothing."

Flavius nodded, though the voice still echoed in his mind. Help me. The words clung to him, refusing to fade. His throat was dry, his thoughts a jumbled mess. He wanted to argue, to demand answers, but the terror in Caius's eyes stopped him.

Caius released him and turned his back to the door, his shoulders tense. "We guard. That's all we do. We don't listen to voices. We don't ask questions. That's the rule."

Flavius nodded again, his hands shaking as he sheathed his blade. The silence stretched on, oppressive and suffocating. He stared at the door, the shadows around it rippling as though alive. He tried to tell himself it was just his imagination, but deep down, he knew better.

The scratching didn't return. The voice didn't speak again. But the plea lingered, echoing in his bones.

Help me.
It was more than a cry for help. It was a promise—a warning. Something was inside that cell, and it wasn't done reaching out.

Chapter 9

The Voice

Joshua sat cross-legged at the edge of the riverbank, the moonlight casting long, silver beams across the flowing water. Shadows swirled and twisted around him like living ink, pulled toward him as if drawn by a magnetic force. Beside him, barely visible in the low light, was Beris—a four-inch-tall figure whose very existence flickered between worlds. When he was still, he looked like an intricately carved doll, but in motion, he flowed like the shadows he travelled through—a small creature embedded in the Dark Matter, constantly phasing in and out of visibility.

It had taken months for Joshua to finally convince Beris to show him how to perform this ritual—the one that would allow him to hear everything within the Dark Matter, the one that promised to unveil secrets hidden in the deepest crevices of reality. At first, Beris had warned him, his tiny voice tinged with urgency, telling him about the dangers of trying to peer too far into the shadows, into the Dark Matter—of pulling at threads that should be left untouched. But Joshua's fascination was unrelenting.

Now, as Beris hovered by the young boy's side, his body glowing faintly with an eerie, otherworldly light, Joshua could feel Beris's excitement mingling with an edge of fear.

'Okay, kid,' Beris whispered, trying to keep his voice steady though it wavered like a thin branch in a storm. 'Last chance to back out. You sure you remember how to start this? Or do you need a cheat sheet?'

He perched on a rock, leaning over Joshua's shoulder, the tips of his tiny fingers tracing the air above the glyphs drawn in the dirt. The glyphs were different from the others they had used—more intricate, more alive. They pulsed with a faint, throbbing blue—a blue that didn't just reflect earthly light but seemed to consume it, drawing all warmth and colour into its depths. It was like staring into the eye of a storm that hungered for more.

Joshua nodded, acknowledging Beris's question, his eyes narrowing onto the symbols marked out on the ground, each one sharp and precise. Every breath felt laboured as if he were pulling in the weight of the shadows themselves. A bead of sweat ran down his face—not from exertion but from the electric tension in the air.

He took a deep breath and, with trembling fingers, reached for the small silver dagger beside him. Its blade already reflected the eerie light of the glyphs.

Beris leaned closer, his whole body tense as a coiled spring. 'Just remember,' he muttered, his voice dropping to a near-whisper as if the night itself might be eavesdropping, 'this isn't like the other rituals. You're not just tapping into some local shadow magic here. You're listening in on... well, everything.'

He paused, his small face tightening as he cast a wary glance at the shadows that began to thicken around them, like black silk threads weaving an ever-tighter cocoon. 'I've never gone this deep. Not really. You could... hear things you're not ready for. And let's be real—you're probably not ready for any of this.'

Joshua's heart hammered in his chest, a rhythm that matched the pulsing glyphs at his feet. He understood what Beris meant—this ritual wasn't just forbidden; it was a doorway into the unknown, a plunge into shadows no one was meant to touch. And for the first time, the intent wasn't just to see what was possible; it was to draw power into himself, to bridge a gap between realms.

Beris had only mentioned it once in passing, calling it 'stupidly reckless'. And Joshua, of course, had to do it.

'Different is good,' Joshua said, his voice barely more than a whisper. Without hesitation and in one swift motion, he sliced his palm open, letting warm blood flow freely over the earth.

The glyphs seemed to come alive at once, greedily drinking in the offering. The blue glow morphed to a deep throbbing crimson, like the veins of an ancient creature coming to life. The world shuddered. The shadows around him didn't just gather; they convulsed, like angry serpents, wrapping themselves around his body, tightening as if trying to draw out more from him—more blood, more energy, more... everything.

Beris's face twisted into a nervous grin, his tiny eyes wide. 'Yep. Totally normal. Nothing to see here. Just a kid bleeding on ancient runes and awakening the who-knows-what.'

He paused for a moment and shook his head in disbelief. 'And in case you were wondering, Joshua, no, I don't have a clue how to put this genie back in its bottle. So, let's just hope this works out for the best.'

But beneath the sarcasm was genuine terror. He kept glancing over his shoulder as if expecting the darkness to reach out and pluck him away at any moment.

Joshua ignored Beris's attempts at humour; he knew his friend well enough to recognise that jokes meant danger. But tonight, nothing could sway him. He could already feel the shadows closing in, their touch cold and familiar, like he'd felt them a thousand times before.

But they weren't what he sought.

Deeper than them, deeper than the black tendrils curling around his limbs and tugging at his mind, was something else—the voice.

The ritual circle pulsed with life. The glyphs seemed to writhe under his touch, their lines twisting and shifting as though alive, drinking deeply of his blood with insatiable thirst. They created a lattice of light and shadow that hovered just above the ground. The crimson glow bathed Joshua's face in an otherworldly light, and for a moment, he thought he could see faces swirling within it—distorted, wailing faces, mouths open in silent screams. But he couldn't let them distract him. He had to focus. He had to find the voice that lurked beyond all this madness, calling to him in dreams and rituals like a half-remembered song.

'Joshua, I don't like this...' Beris's voice was small, a rare tremor in its usual steadiness. 'It feels... it feels like we're being watched. And not the friendly, "I'll wave to you from across the street" kind of watch. More like... dinner.'

Joshua continued chanting the words Beris had taught him—ancient phrases, dense and heavy, each syllable dragging the world around him deeper into shadow. The earth trembled beneath him, a low rumbling like the growl of a beast just waking up. The shadows tightened, their tendrils curling around his throat and limbs like vines growing at an impossible speed. He felt the whispers merging into his thoughts, promising power, strength, and visions no human eyes had ever seen. But he brushed them aside. They were just noise, distractions. The voice was what mattered. That's all that really mattered.

The shadows surged, coiling tighter like a storm gathering strength, their movements liquid yet alive, each tendril dripping with an unnatural hunger. They slithered over his skin, their movements serpentine and deliberate, coiling around his arms like sentient vines, each touch colder than the last. At first, their touch was just a chill, a coldness that seeped into his skin. But as they tightened their grip, the cold grew sharp—biting, like stinging nettles digging into his flesh.

Joshua felt them wrap around his throat, squeezing, and he struggled for air, each breath harder to take than the last. It was as if the shadows were filling his lungs, weighing them down, and the more he breathed, the deeper they reached.

The smell hit him next—thick and rotten, like the decay of something long dead and buried. It hung in the air, clogging his senses and turning every breath into a struggle. Joshua gagged, bile rising in his throat as the fetid stench clawed its way into his nose. The air tasted metallic, like copper or iron, each breath leaving a rusty tang on his tongue that made his mouth water with nausea. He could feel it at the back of his throat, a sharpness that scratched as he inhaled, as if he were sucking in shards of metal.

Suddenly, his skin felt raw, as if the darkness were scraping at his very bones. The pressure of the shadows became overwhelming like heavy chains pulling him down, the weight growing unbearable. Panic flashed in his eyes, and he tried to shake them off, but the shadows only tightened in response, digging into his flesh like talons. They burrowed into him, seeming to slither beneath the surface of his skin, probing deeper, seeking to tear something out of him that lay hidden deep inside.

Joshua's vision swam, spots of black and red dancing before his eyes. The whispers grew louder, no longer gentle promises but furious, jagged demands that ripped through his mind like serrated blades. He felt the tendrils slither over his face, oily and wet, wrapping around his eyes, pressing down, trying to blind him. He clawed at them desperately, his fingers sinking into their slimy, writhing forms, but it was like tearing at a swarm of slick, living worms.

The shadows tightened in triumph, their darkness growing heavier and more suffocating, a crushing tide that surged up to drag him under. He choked on the taste of rot, his stomach turning as the stench of decay thickened, and the world around him spiralled into a nightmarish blackness.

Then it came—a faint murmur threading through the chaos, soft yet undeniable. The voice carried the weight of desperation, raw and broken, each syllable like a shard of glass slicing through the darkness. Each word seemed to pulse with agony, yet it was familiar to him, like a dream that wouldn't leave him, like something buried deep within his very bones.

'Joshua...' the voice whispered, broken and raw, and Joshua's heart stuttered.

It was the voice that had haunted every ritual, every shadow-drenched night. He could almost see the man behind the voice—gaunt, with eyes that burned like coals, chained in darkness somewhere far away, somewhere he couldn't reach. And yet, he was certain he knew the man. He just didn't know how.

Joshua leaned into the voice, pushing deeper into the shadows that clawed at him, hoping to hear more, to see more. 'Who are you?' he whispered, though it felt like screaming into an abyss. 'Where are you?'

Beris's form flickered, his terror snapping into full-blown panic as he phased in and out of view, struggling to maintain his shape against the overwhelming tide of power. 'Joshua, listen to me,' he shouted, though his tiny voice was nearly swallowed by the roaring shadows. 'Joshua, whatever you think you're hearing, it's not worth this,' Beris hissed, his tiny hands gripping at the fabric of Joshua's sleeve. 'You're meddling with things that don't care if they destroy you. Break the circle. Now.'

Joshua's vision was filled with darkness, writhing and twisting in on itself, growing deeper and colder as he pushed further in. The shadows began to change, their whispers turning from seductive promises to guttural threats. The tendrils tightened around his limbs and throat, squeezing, pulling, trying to drag him into their depths. He could feel their cold, oily touch seeping into his skin, filling his lungs, threatening to drown him.

'Damn it, Joshua!' Beris cried, trying to climb Joshua's sleeve, to pull him away from the shadows with all his strength—small but fiercely determined. 'This isn't some game! I can't protect you from... from this!' His tiny voice broke, caught between anger and desperation. 'Don't let them take you like... like they did your father!'

And yet, through all of it, the voice persisted—a beacon calling to him, pulling him across the divide. Joshua could almost feel the chains around the man's wrists, could almost touch the cold stone walls of his prison beneath the ground, somewhere deep in the earth. He felt like he could pull the man toward him and rip him from the darkness.

The darkness clawed at Joshua, closing in like a tomb, yet somewhere in the roiling depths of his mind—beneath the whispers, the sickening stench of decay, and the metallic taste that clung to his tongue—something broke through. A moment of clarity, thin as a thread, cut through the oppressive noise. He latched onto it, focusing with all his might, and the world around him—the shadows constricting his limbs, the howling voices—faded to a distant hum.

Beris's frantic voice became an echo, barely discernible, like a tiny bell ringing in an endless void. 'Joshua! Joshua, for the love of the gods, STOP!' But the sound felt miles away, disconnected from Joshua's mind and body. With a final surge of will, he broke free—not physically but mentally—pushing himself deeper into the dark, beyond the shadows that consumed him, beyond the voices that taunted him, beyond everything... until he was no longer in his body but somewhere else entirely.

He was suddenly transported to a place deeper than any shadow he'd ever known—a realm so black, so silent, that even the spirits seemed to fear treading there. Joshua stood in the Dark Matter, in its deepest heart, a place beyond the reach of time and light. The ground beneath him was cold and smooth, the texture of polished stone, yet somehow endless, disappearing into the void. He looked around but saw nothing—no walls, no sky, no horizon—only pure, impenetrable black.

It was as if the darkness was alive, watching him, swallowing everything he was. And then he saw it—a single piece of furniture against
the endless void with an unnatural glow, like a lamp floating next to
it to illuminate its presence.

A wingback chair, large and imposing, made of dark leather so deeply black it blended into the shadows. It seemed to swallow his small
frame as he took his place in it, drawn to it like a moth to flame. He
felt himself sinking into the chair, its cold leather wrapping around
him, cradling him as though it were sentient. But the real presence in
the room was not the chair—it was the man who suddenly appeared
sitting across from him, whom he only saw once he sat down.

The figure was tall, his features half-hidden by the shadows that
seemed to drape around him like a cloak. There was something ancient in his bearing, something far more powerful than any force
Joshua had felt before. Though the man was still, a pulsing energy
radiated from him like a storm trapped within human form. His eyes
were sharp, piercing through the darkness, burning with a light that
felt like truth itself.

Joshua could not look away, and he realised in that moment that they
were not strangers. They had met before—maybe in dreams, maybe
across lifetimes—but there was a familiarity, an unspoken connection, that bound them across the endless dark.

They exchanged no words. They didn't need to. They spoke through
the eyes, through a knowing—conversing in thoughts more profound
than language, deeper than sound. Joshua's heart raced, and in that
silence, they shared something profound, a mutual understanding
that he could not yet comprehend. But there was a sense of destiny,
of purpose, that grew between them like a flame being kindled in the
pitch-black dark.

After a long pause, Joshua's voice finally broke the silence, quiet yet
strong. 'Who... are you?'

The man's lips curved into a faint, enigmatic smile, and when he
spoke, his voice was like a whisper that had travelled through a thou-

sand lifetimes to reach this point. 'My name,' he said, his eyes steady on Joshua's, 'is Yehoshua.'

And with that name, the world seemed to ripple, the very fabric of reality bending around the sound.

'I need you to stay focused, Joshua,' Yehoshua continued, his voice calm yet filled with an urgency that Joshua felt deep in his bones. 'I chose you long ago to complete a task for me. I caused your existence because I have a plan... and I need your help.'

Joshua felt his breath catch in his throat, the weight of the moment pressing down on him like the gravity of a thousand worlds. He couldn't speak, couldn't move—he was ensnared by Yehoshua's gaze, pulled into the depths of his eyes, which seemed to reflect all of creation.

'What do you need me to do?' Joshua finally whispered.

Yehoshua's gaze softened, a sad understanding in his eyes, as if he could see both the burden he was placing on Joshua and the path that lay before him.

'You must deliver a message,' Yehoshua said, his voice low and urgent, 'to a priest named Bussi. He holds the key to my freedom—though he doesn't know it yet. I am imprisoned, trapped beneath layers of stone and magic, but my chains are spread across the multiverse. And somewhere, Bussi holds the key to freeing me.'

Joshua's brow furrowed in confusion. 'But... how do I find him? Which Bussi do I need? What world is he in?'

Yehoshua's face darkened with something like regret. 'I do not know. I cannot see clearly enough to tell you that. The multiverse is endless, and the shadows have blinded me,' Yehoshua admitted, his tone heavy with regret. 'You'll need to cross worlds and unravel timelines until you find him—the one Bussi who can set me free.'

Joshua nodded, the enormity of the task settling on his shoulders, the fear and excitement merging into a dizzying storm in his chest. He could feel Yehoshua's strength pouring into him, filling him with a sense of purpose, a calling.

'But how will I know?' Joshua asked, his voice small. 'How will I know which version of him is the right one?'

Yehoshua leaned back, the shadows shifting around him, and though his voice remained steady, there was a flicker of something beneath the surface—a glimpse of the pain, the desperation that drove him. 'You will know, Joshua. You have my blood in your veins, my purpose in your soul. You will feel it, like a compass pointing home.'

Joshua tried to hold onto the moment, to grasp the clarity that Yehoshua was offering him, but it was like clutching water—slipping away even as he tried to hold on. He opened his mouth to ask another question, to dive deeper into the truth he could feel on the edge of his understanding—but suddenly, Yehoshua's form began to flicker, his edges dissolving into the dark.

'Wait!' Joshua called out, leaning forward, reaching for Yehoshua, for the truth he felt slipping away.

But then, through the chaos, another voice—a familiar, desperate voice—broke through like a blade of light cutting through the dark.

'Joshua!'

Zivah's voice, raw with terror, cut through the shadows, shattering the trance. She stood on the edge of the ritual circle, her hand outstretched, but held back as if by an invisible force.

'Joshua, listen to me! You have to stop this!'

Joshua's eyes snapped open, the trance fracturing. 'Mum?' His voice cracked.

And in that instant, the glyphs exploded into a whirlwind of sparks and smoke. The lattice of light and shadow disintegrated, and the roar of the ritual was swallowed by the rushing river, leaving Joshua gasping on the ground, the world suddenly too bright and real.

'I can't just stop,' Joshua said, his voice trembling. 'I need to know who I am... what I'm meant to do. And if I don't... if I don't explore this, if I don't try... then I'll never know, will I?'

Beris, regaining some composure, hovered beside them, his expression unreadable. 'He's got a point,' Beris said softly. 'Every Gifted one has to test their limits eventually. Better now than... later. When he's not ready.'

'Limits?' Zivah snapped, turning her furious eyes on Beris. 'And who's going to teach him those limits? You? The one who's already pushed him so far into this mess that he nearly—' She stopped, fighting back a sob. 'I trusted you to protect him, not... not lead him into whatever this is!'

Beris sighed, looking away, and for once, he seemed to have no retort. 'Look, Zivah,' he said finally, his voice softer. 'I never wanted to hurt him. I just... I want him to be ready. Ready for what's coming.'

'And what's coming?' Zivah whispered, holding Joshua tighter, her voice shaking with desperation. 'What could possibly be worth this? Worth risking him?'

Beris's face darkened, and he glanced at Joshua, who could still feel the phantom of the shadows wrapping around him. 'More than either of you know,' Beris muttered. 'More than you can see right now.'

Zivah rushed forward, grabbing Joshua's arms, searching his face frantically. 'What were you doing?' she demanded, her voice trembling with both fury and fear. She tore a strip from her sleeve to bandage his bleeding hand. 'What did you think you were doing? You're too young for this—it's too dangerous!'

Joshua met her gaze, his eyes still unfocused. The world felt distant, dreamlike. He could still hear the voice, faint and fading, but there.

'I had to hear... him,' he whispered. 'I had to... find him.'

Zivah's eyes filled with tears as she held him close, her fingers gripping his arms like anchors. 'I lost your father to this darkness,' Zivah choked out, her voice fraying with fear and fury. 'I won't lose you too. You have to promise me, Joshua—promise me you'll stop before it's too late.'

Joshua nodded, though the weight of the promise meant little to him. Because beneath the river's current and the soft rustling of leaves, he could still hear the voice calling to him from the shadows, begging him to return. Somewhere deep beneath layers of stone and magic, a man was waiting for him.

And Joshua, no matter how much he tried to ignore it, couldn't help but listen.

As they walked away from the riverbank, the shadows began to recede, sliding back into the earth like oil sinking into the soil. The glyphs faded into the night, their glow extinguished, but the darkness they left behind hung thick and heavy, like a promise unspoken—a whisper that some things, once heard, cannot so easily be forgotten.

In the distance, where the river's silver sheen met the darkened trees, Beris dissolved into shadow, leaving only a faint ripple in the air, as though he had never been there at all. Just before the silence swallowed the night whole, Joshua heard it—a whisper, faint yet unyielding, calling to him from the edges of existence.

Promising secrets. Promising strength.

Promising more.

Chapter 10

Caius & Flavius

Their torches flickered wildly, their faint flames battling the oppressive darkness. Shadows danced erratically across the damp, crumbling stone walls as if synchronised. The air was damp, laced with the scent of mildew and the faint tang of something metallic, something very wrong.

The silence that filled the corridor was palpable. Flavius cautiously proceeded down the corridor, his heart pounding as he followed Caius further down the passageway. They hadn't been here in what felt like an eternity, but the unease had returned, more pronounced than ever.

Caius walked ahead, his confident stride reduced to measured steps. His shoulders, usually squared with purpose, were hunched slightly forward. Flavius couldn't miss the tension in his movements nor how Caius's hand hovered closer to his blade than usual. The ancient iron door loomed before them, its surface etched with faint, jagged marks that seemed to shift in the torchlight. Rust clung to its jagged edges, but the air around it hummed faintly, like an unseen force pulsing in tandem with their heartbeats. It felt alive—waiting—holding its breath as though aware of their presence. Flavius felt that familiar, gnawing dread crawl up his spine, a memory of the last time they'd been here whispering in the back of his mind. He tried to suppress it, but the unease clung like a shadow he couldn't shake. His grip tightened around his blade, just as it had before.

'Just like last time,' Flavius muttered, his voice barely audible. 'I can feel it. Whatever's in there... it seems to be getting worse.'

Caius didn't respond straight away. He paused, staring at the door, his jaw tight. 'You're imagining things,' he said, but his voice lacked conviction.

A sudden crack shattered the silence, sharp and hollow, echoing from behind the door. Flavius froze mid-step, his breath catching in his throat. The sound was followed by a low groan of strained metal as though something heavy stirred just beyond the barrier. Both men froze. Flavius's hand instinctively reached for his blade while Caius's eyes darted to the door. The sound had come from inside.

'It's waking up,' Flavius whispered, his voice trembling, betraying the cold sweat trickling down his back. He gripped his blade a little tighter, its hilt slick against his damp palms.

The door rattled slightly—just once—enough to remind them both of the power hidden behind it. The ground beneath them trembled, barely noticeable but enough to make them glance at each other, their fear now unspoken but shared.

'Do we report this?' Flavius asked.

Caius hesitated, then muttered, 'We don't leave our post, Flavius,' his voice low, barely audible. 'But... stay sharp. Something's different tonight.' But even he knew this time was different.

The silence that followed was heavier than before. Something had shifted, and they both knew whatever was behind that door wasn't just stirring—it was waking, and the fragile barrier between them felt thinner than ever.

Chapter 11

The Order of the Hidden Cross

Yehoshua of Nazareth was dead—or so the world believed. Sealed in a cold, dark tomb, his mutilated body lay shrouded in silence while his followers scattered like dust before the wind. But the stillness was a lie. Beneath the stone, something stirred—a shadow of a truth so dark, so damning, it would demand centuries of blood to conceal.

Joseph of Arimathea stood outside the tomb, his hand trembling as he clutched the iron key. The heavy stone had been rolled across the entrance days before, sealing away a body and the truth. He had watched the man hang on the cross, had seen his blood soak the earth beneath him. Yehoshua had died—of that, Joseph had been certain. But now, something else gnawed at the edges of his mind, a whisper that wouldn't leave him.

When the stone was finally pushed aside, the sight that greeted him dropped him to his knees.

Yehoshua wasn't dead. He wasn't alive either—not as they had expected. Yehoshua's body was a grotesque shadow of its former self. His once olive skin had taken on a sickly shade of white, entangled with the unforgettable bluish-grey shade of death. His lips now cracked, dried blood settling around their edges. His wounds, wrapped in linen, oozed a thick, blackened pus, mixing with the dried blood that had long ago clotted but never fully healed. Punctured by nails, his hands were curled inward, stiff and gnarled as if he were still gripping something invisible.

His chest barely rose with each ragged breath, the sound of it wet and phlegmy, a grotesque rattle that seemed to scrape against his throat. Beneath his eyes, dark purple bruises stretched like shadows across his gaunt face. His eyelids occasionally fluttered, revealing bloodshot eyes that seemed too heavy to fully open. Still, when they did, they glistened with the sheen of delirium.

There were moments, fleeting and almost imperceptible, when his body shuddered violently as if reliving the agony of the torture he endured. A low, guttural moan, almost inhuman, escaped his lips, but it was faint—so faint Joseph had to strain to hear it, and when he did, it sent a cold shiver down his spine.

Joseph staggered back, the stench of decay thick in the damp tomb air, clinging to his skin like an accusation. He had expected the healer, the teacher—the man who had walked on water and spoken of love with divine authority. What he found instead was a broken shell, trapped between death and something unspeakably worse. The sight unravelled his faith, one fragile thread at a time.

It wasn't a resurrection, not in the way the scriptures foretold. There had been no divine spark, no heavenly choir. This was something else. Yehoshua was alive, yes, but barely. His skin was cold to the touch, his eyes sunken. A great shudder passed through his body as if it had come back from the grave with pieces of death still clinging to it.

Joseph recoiled, unsure of what he was seeing. 'Lord?' he whispered, his voice breaking in the cold night air. 'What... what is this?'

But there were no answers, only weak breaths and the terrifying knowledge that what lay before him was neither a man nor a god.

The resurrection story would soon sweep through Jerusalem like wildfire, but only a handful of souls would know the truth.

Over the next few days, as Yehoshua lay hidden in a cave, tended to by Joseph, this strange story of resurrection began to emerge. The disciples, who had scattered in fear after Yehoshua's crucifixion, returned to Jerusalem only to be confronted by these strange rumours. Whispers spread through the city that Yehoshua had risen from the dead, just as he had foretold. Some claimed to have seen him walking the streets, his face aglow with divine power. Others swore they had spoken to him, touched his wounds.

At first, the disciples dismissed the rumours as wild fabrications, stories borne out of grief and desperation. But as the stories persisted, they began to wonder. What if it was true? What if Yehoshua really had returned from the grave, defeating death itself? The pressure from the crowds, the growing myth, became too much for them to fight. And so, reluctantly, they embraced the story—He is risen!

In reality, Yehoshua had not risen in the way the rumours suggested. He had not ascended to heaven in a blaze of glory. He was hidden away, recovering from the torment of crucifixion. His body was weak and broken, but his spirit—his divinity—remained intact. He was alive, but not for the world to see. For the disciples, it was easier to let the people believe the myth. It gave them hope. It gave them strength. And so, the story of the Resurrection was born—a convenient lie to keep the faith alive.

While whispers of Yehoshua's miraculous return to life began to spread, Saul of Tarsus found himself on his way to Damascus. A

Zealot and a man known for his vicious persecution of the early followers of Yehoshua, Saul was determined to stamp out their blasphemous teachings. Saul had been on the road to Damascus, his heart filled with hatred, when the first rumours reached his ears. The disciples are going to try to kill you on the road.

But Saul, ever the cunning strategist, heard something else hidden beneath the stories—the thread of a secret he could use. That Yehoshua was still alive.

Saul arrived in Damascus under the guise of a convert. He claimed to have had a divine experience, a revelation that had changed his heart. None other than Christ himself appeared to him, giving him the specific task of starting his church. But those who truly knew Saul and had witnessed the cold steel of his eyes understood that the man's ambitions ran far deeper than religious fervour.

The disciples, wary of Saul's reputation, were not easily swayed. Peter, James, and John all rejected Saul, sensing something false in his words. The man had been hunting them not long ago, and now he wanted to join them? It felt wrong. They sent Saul away, refusing to accept him and his story.

But Saul was undeterred. If the disciples did not believe him, he would take matters into his own hands. He began to track the rumours, following the whispering crowds until he heard something that piqued his interest—a tale of Yehoshua still alive but hidden. That was when Saul's true plan began to form.

Saul returned to Jerusalem, still pretending to be a convert. He sought out the remnants of Yehoshua's followers, bribing informants and threatening those who kept the secret. Eventually, he found what he had been looking for: Yehoshua, hidden in a tomb, alive but barely clinging to life. Joseph of Arimathea, who had given Yehoshua a resting place after the crucifixion, had been secretly tending to him, keeping him hidden from the world.

He found Joseph of Arimathea in the dead of night, his face hidden beneath the hood of a cloak. 'I've heard whispers,' Saul said, his voice low and dangerous. 'Whispers of a man who should be dead but isn't.' Joseph's blood ran cold. He had done his best to keep Yehoshua hidden, to protect him while his body slowly recovered from its ordeal. But Saul's presence here could mean only one thing: the secret had leaked. Someone had talked.

'It's true, then,' Saul continued, stepping closer. 'He lives.'

'Not as you think,' Joseph replied, his voice trembling. 'He was... it was an accident; they thought he died. He wasn't resurrected. He wasn't brought back by God. He had never really died.'

Saul's eyes glittered with something far more dangerous than mere interest. 'That's what makes it even better, Joseph. If they believe he conquered death, then his followers will grow. His message will spread. But if the truth comes out—if they know it was just a mistake and he just survived—everything falls apart.'

Saul's mind worked quickly, faster than Joseph could keep up. He saw the opportunity, the power that could come from controlling this narrative. Yehoshua's supposed resurrection could be the spark for something much larger—a movement, an empire. But Yehoshua was now a liability, a fragile piece of flesh that could ruin the divine story.

Saul of Tarsus stood over the motionless body of Yehoshua, his hand trembling as it gripped the blood-stained dagger. His heart raced with a mixture of triumph and terror. He had plunged the blade deep into Yehoshua's side, sure that this would end it—that the heretic who claimed to be the Son of God would finally meet death like any mortal man. And yet, as Saul stared down at Yehoshua's still form, horror began to dawn upon him.

Yehoshua had not died.

Blood poured from the wound, but it wasn't the vibrant red of life—it was a thick, almost tar-like substance, darker than it should have been, congealing even as it left his body. Yehoshua's muscles twitched involuntarily, his body spasming as if trying to react to the violence it had endured. His eyes, still half-closed, flickered, but they did not focus on anything—glazed, like a man lost in some nightmarish fog.

The gaping wound Saul had inflicted on his side revealed flesh that should have been healing by now, but instead, it festered, swollen, and inflamed. His skin stretched tight, grotesque, over the edges of the puncture, almost as if the flesh itself were pulling away from the wound, recoiling from the blade. Yehoshua's breath hitched, a gurgling rasp escaping his throat, and a thin stream of blood, mixed with saliva, trickled down his chin.

The tomb echoed with the sound of Yehoshua's agony—a muffled, guttural groan, as though the weight of death clung to him but refused to claim him. His body, pale and cold, lay limp but alive, trembling as if every nerve was still alight with the torment of crucifixion.

Saul stood frozen momentarily, staring at the black blood pooling beneath the Messiah. It smelled of rot, the sharp tang of iron mingling with the unmistakable stench of death. But Yehoshua, impossibly, still lived.

This man, this humble carpenter who had wandered through Galilee preaching love and forgiveness, was something far more than Saul had ever imagined. He was no mere prophet. He was something far beyond human comprehension, something terrible and eternal. Yehoshua was a god, trapped in human form, and death had no hold over him.

Saul's heart thundered as realisation struck with cold precision—he had failed. The blade that had felled countless men had merely wounded Yehoshua, leaving him trapped in a grotesque limbo. The blackened blood pooling beneath the Messiah carried the stench of death, yet he lived, clinging to life with a force that defied logic, nature, and Saul's will. This was no ordinary man. This was something beyond understanding, something Saul could neither kill nor, up until now, control.

Panic surged through Saul's veins, followed closely by fury. He had staked everything on this act of betrayal—everything. If Yehoshua continued to live, if word got out that Saul had failed, everything he had planned would fall apart. And worse—if Yehoshua rose again, if he regained his strength, the world would know Saul's true intentions.

He could not let that happen.

But Saul's mind had always been sharp, calculating. He was nothing if not adaptable. His greatest strength lay not in brute force but in manipulation. If he could not kill Yehoshua, he would find another way—a way to control him, to imprison him.

He took a deep breath, forcing himself to think. He had to act quickly, but not rashly. His initial plan had failed, but there was still an opportunity here—an opportunity far greater than Saul had first realised.

Rather than being a failure, Yehoshua's survival could become Saul's greatest weapon.

His eyes darted toward Joseph of Arimathea, who stood frozen in the corner of the tomb, watching the scene with wide, terrified eyes. Joseph had witnessed everything—the knife, the blood, Yehoshua's strange, unnatural survival. He knew the truth, but he was no zealot like Saul. Joseph had always been compassionate, a man who followed Yehoshua's teachings with a quiet dignity. He could be manipulated.

Saul turned toward Joseph, his mind already weaving a new narrative. He wiped the dagger clean on his cloak and stepped closer, his voice cold and commanding. 'Let them believe he rose,' Saul said, his voice sharp with conviction. 'A divine ascension will inspire faith like nothing else. But the truth? The truth stays with us. We'll keep him where no one can see—not alive, not dead, but ours.'

Joseph recoiled, his eyes wide with horror. 'Keep him? What do you mean, Saul? He's alive! This... this is the Messiah! We cannot keep him imprisoned like some animal!'

Saul's lips curled into a cruel smile. 'We must, Joseph. Don't you see? His presence—his true presence—will destroy everything. Suppose the people find out that Yehoshua did not conquer death. In that case, their faith would shatter if he simply survived through some accident of nature. They believe in a resurrection. They need to believe in it. If they learn the truth, it will all come crumbling down.'

Joseph took a step back, shaking his head in disbelief. 'But Saul... you tried to kill him. You stabbed him.'

'And he lived,' Saul hissed, his eyes narrowing. 'Don't you see? He is too dangerous. Yehoshua's true power is beyond our comprehension, beyond anything we can control. If he ever recovers, if he regains his strength, he could undo everything we've worked for. No, Joseph. We will hide him away. We will make sure that no one ever sees him again.'

Joseph's face paled. He looked down at Yehoshua, lying helpless and wounded on the cold stone slab. The man who had been their teacher, their hope, was now little more than a shell of his former self. His breathing was shallow, his body weak. There was no sign of the godlike figure the people had come to worship.

But Joseph still saw the humanity in him. He couldn't go along with Saul's plan. He couldn't let this happen.

'I won't do it, Saul,' Joseph whispered, his voice trembling. 'I won't be part of this. This is wrong. This is... blasphemy.'

Joseph's hands trembled as Saul's words echoed in the cold, hollow chamber. The tomb had once been a place of silent reverence, where the broken body of Yehoshua lay in the throes of death's grip. Now, it felt suffocating, like the weight of all creation had been placed on Joseph's chest. His breath hitched, his eyes fixed on the motionless figure of Yehoshua, barely alive, barely human, yet unmistakably divine.

He could still remember the day Yehoshua spoke to him, his voice filled with compassion and quiet authority, his words carrying the weight of a truth that could heal nations. Love thy neighbour as thyself, Yehoshua had said. Do not be afraid, Joseph, for the Kingdom of God is near.

And yet, here Joseph stood, watching the very man who had healed the sick, comforted the broken, now reduced to a fragile shell. Was this truly the Messiah? Could he allow this divine being, this hope for the world, to be imprisoned? His heart pounded in his chest. Every fibre of his soul screamed for him to kneel beside Yehoshua, to cradle his broken body and protect him from the evil that now stood before him.

But then there was Saul.

Saul, whose cold, calculating gaze held no warmth, no light. His words carried the weight of a threat Joseph couldn't ignore. The dagger gleamed in Saul's hand, still slick with Yehoshua's blood, a blood that had flowed too freely. Saul had failed to kill Yehoshua, but Joseph knew he wouldn't hesitate to kill someone else. And if Joseph stood in his way, the next dagger might find his own flesh.

'Do you really want to die, Joseph?' Saul's voice was soft now, almost kind, but the venom beneath it was unmistakable. 'Do you want to be buried here, forgotten by the world, just like him?'

Joseph's heart pounded, each beat a hammer blow against his resolve. Loyalty warred with terror, his mind spinning with the impossible choice before him. He saw the path of betrayal stretch out like a scar—a future where his cowardice stained Yehoshua's suffering. Yet martyrdom loomed just as grimly. If he defied Saul, who would shield Yehoshua from the darkness coiling around him? Who would protect the Messiah if Joseph became another lifeless body in this tomb? If Joseph died, the last of those who truly cared for Yehoshua would be gone. And Saul... Saul would win.

He felt the weight of Yehoshua's presence beside him, lying helpless on the cold slab. His breathing was shallow, his body broken, yet there was something else—something unyielding in the man's stillness, as if Yehoshua's spirit was waiting, biding its time. Joseph clenched his fists. The Messiah was alive, but for how long? Saul would see to it that Yehoshua's suffering never ended.

For a brief moment, Joseph wondered if Yehoshua could hear them—if the man who had walked on water, who had commanded the storm to cease, still had the strength to hear their plans of betrayal. Could Yehoshua sense the conflict in Joseph's heart? Could he, in his divine awareness, understand the torment Joseph faced?

What do I do, Lord? Joseph's thoughts screamed in the silence of the tomb. How can I betray you like this?

'Joseph,' Saul's voice cut through the darkness, harsh and insistent. 'We're running out of time. Decide now. Will you help me, or do I bury you alongside him?'

Joseph's gaze flickered to Saul, then back to Yehoshua. His lips trembled, but he spoke no words. He didn't need to. The answer had already formed in the cold, tight grip of fear.

'I... I will help you,' Joseph whispered, each word tasting like ash in his mouth.

'Good,' Saul replied, a slow, satisfied smile spreading across his face. 'Then we are agreed. Yehoshua's resurrection will be our truth, our story to control. And no one will ever know what truly happened here.'

But as Saul turned away to begin making arrangements, Joseph lingered beside Yehoshua. His heart was heavy, his mind swirling with regret, shame, and a small flicker of defiance. He couldn't leave Yehoshua like this—bound in the shadows, hidden away from the world. No matter what Saul said, Joseph knew he had to do something, even if it was small, even dangerous perhaps.

Joseph stood over Yehoshua, watching as the blood pooled beneath him. The smell of decay clung to the tomb's walls like a living thing, and for the first time, Joseph felt the full weight of what Saul had done—what he had allowed. He could feel the bile rising in his throat, the bitter taste of guilt mingling with the stench of death. How had it come to this?

He knelt closer, drawn by a force he couldn't explain, as if some part of Yehoshua's suffering pulled at him. Joseph could see it in Yehoshua's eyes—the dim awareness of pain, the slow, helpless blink of a man too weak to even turn his head. His once strong hands, hands that had blessed children and broken bread for the multitudes, now lay shrivelled and limp, useless.

Joseph's heart ached. Yehoshua had once radiated life, a quiet, gentle strength that could calm storms and heal the sick. But now, he was a broken vessel, his body a grotesque parody of the divine light he once carried. And Joseph—Joseph had helped to imprison him.

A faint, raspy breath escaped Yehoshua's lips. In that small sound, Joseph could almost hear the unspoken words: Why have you abandoned me?

In that brief moment of stillness, Joseph made a silent vow. I will not abandon you.

He couldn't defy Saul openly—not yet—but there would be small ways to resist. Perhaps he could find herbs to ease Yehoshua's pain or whisper words of encouragement into his ear when the guards were gone. Perhaps there were hidden allies within the city, other followers who could help Yehoshua escape this fate. He didn't know what the future held, but he wouldn't let fear be his master forever.

Joseph stood and, for the first time, met Saul's gaze without flinching. 'I'll help you, but I want to be the one who tends to him. No one else should be near him.'

Saul frowned but shrugged, dismissing the request as inconsequential. 'Fine. Do whatever you need. Just make sure he doesn't get any stronger.'

Joseph bowed his head, concealing the flicker of rebellion in his heart. 'As you wish.'

'Good,' Saul said, his voice dripping with cold satisfaction. 'Then we are agreed. The people will believe that Yehoshua has risen, that he had ascended to heaven in triumph. But we will know the truth. We will keep him hidden, weakened. Forever.'

And so, the Order of the Hidden Cross was born—a brotherhood forged in shadows, lies, and blood. Saul's ambitions drew men as ruthless as himself—Roman soldiers, Jewish Pharisees and Sadducee collaborators, travelling practitioners of dark arts—occultists who had delved into the mysteries of life and death, all seeking ways to control him. Together, they would form an unholy alliance bound by a single mission: to keep Yehoshua hidden, imprisoned, and powerless.

At first, they tried simple methods—herbs, wines, anything to keep Yehoshua sedated. But as his strength slowly returned, Saul realised that Yehoshua, even in his broken state, was far stronger than any man. The feeble potions they used to dull his senses were not enough. They needed something more substantial, something more ancient, more powerful.

And so, the Order scoured the lands, searching for witches, shamans, and healers who understood the deepest mysteries of the human soul. They gathered the knowledge of forgotten empires, experimenting with dark alchemy and forbidden magic. Over the centuries, they perfected their craft, creating a powerful potion that could keep even a god in a state of near-death—a concoction that would keep Yehoshua's mind clouded and his body frail.

As Yehoshua lay hidden in a secret chamber, deep beneath Rome itself, Saul of Tarsus—now calling himself Paul—began to spread his new vision of Yehoshua's message. But this was not the message of love, compassion, and justice that Yehoshua had taught his disciples. No, Paul's gospel was one of control, of obedience, of submission to the divine authority of the church. His authority.

Paul's teachings became the foundation of what would grow into the Roman Catholic Church, an empire built not on Yehoshua's true teachings but on the lie of his resurrection—a resurrection that had never truly happened.

Paul was not a convert. He was the first Antichrist, a man who had glimpsed the truth of Yehoshua's power and chosen to twist it for his own gain. His letters, his travels, his influence—they all served a single purpose: to establish a Church that would control the minds and hearts of billions for millennia to come.

All the while, Yehoshua remained hidden, his body broken, his mind clouded by the dark potions of the Order. The world believed that Yehoshua had ascended to heaven and that he sat at the right hand of God. But in truth, the man they worshipped as the Son of God lay in a forgotten cell, kept alive by the very men who claimed to serve him.

As the centuries passed, the Order of the Hidden Cross grew in strength and secrecy. Their methods became more refined, and their influence became more insidious. Popes, kings, and emperors all fell under their shadow. Any who sought the truth were silenced, and those within the Church who grew too close to the secret were 'dealt with'.

Even Popes were not safe. Some, who had dared to question the true history of Yehoshua, were quickly 'replaced' by the Order, ensuring that the lie would continue unchallenged.

The Catholic Church, the largest and most powerful institution in the world, stood as a monument to Paul's grand deception. The world worshipped Yehoshua as the Son of God, never knowing that the man they revered was kept sedated and hidden from them, his true message of peace and justice twisted beyond recognition.

The Order of the Hidden Cross remained vigilant, even today. They controlled the Church, not from the pulpits or the altars, but from the shadows. Their influence was vast, and their knowledge of Yehoshua's true fate was passed down through the centuries through whispered rites and forbidden texts.

The world would never know the truth. Not if the Order had anything to say about it.

Beneath the Vatican, in a chamber cloaked in relics of forgotten empires, the man they called Christ began to stir. His frail, broken body shuddered, the ancient potions that had clouded his mind weakening with each passing hour. In the suffocating dark, Yehoshua's thoughts sharpened like blades, cutting through centuries of fog. A promise kindled within him, faint but unyielding: he would rise again.

Somewhere in the depths of his soul, Yehoshua remembered.

He remembered the promise he had made to his followers—that one day, he would return. And as that promise stirred within him, so too did his strength.

The Order knew the day would come when they could no longer contain him. And when that day came, they would face an impossible choice—let the truth be revealed, or destroy him once and for all.

Chapter 12

The Oath

The day they took their oath, the bells of the Vatican tolled loud and clear—a stark contrast to the oppressive silence that would come to define their lives. Paolo and Francesco stood side by side in the Grand Hall, surrounded by towering marble pillars and gilded frescoes that depicted scenes of divine grace and glory. The ceremonial robes they wore were spotless, pure white trimmed with crimson—a sign of the duty they were about to take on. Their faces were tense, their eyes filled with the uncertain fire of men who knew they were entering into something much larger than themselves.

Cardinal Gianni stood before them, draped in gold-embroidered robes, his eyes hard and distant. He towered over them both, a figure who seemed to have no use for compassion. At the altar, he held the ancient tome—the Codex Illuminatus, its worn leather cover engraved with symbols older than Rome itself.

'Today, you become members of the Order of the Hidden Cross,' Gianni intoned, his voice echoing through the cavernous hall. The words carried a cold finality, like the closing of a door that would never open again. 'As such, you take on a burden far heavier than any clergyman has ever known.'

Francesco's heart raced, though he kept his face impassive. He'd heard tales whispered late at night about what the Order truly guarded, but no one ever spoke of it openly. Once you took the oath, there was no way out.

Paolo's hands twitched at his side, betraying his nerves. Francesco glanced at him, their eyes meeting briefly. He could see the unease there, the apprehension. They were about to pledge their lives to a shadow they could only glimpse through stories and half-truths.

'Repeat after me,' Cardinal Gianni continued, opening the Codex. 'I swear to protect the sanctity of the Church. To guard its secrets with my life. To serve the Order, and to keep my silence.'

Paolo's voice wavered as he repeated the words, a strained whisper. Francesco followed, the weight of the words feeling like chains wrapping around him, binding him to something unseen.

Gianni's gaze bore into them. 'And do you swear to give your lives in service to the Order, to protect the faith so that this abomination never sees the light of day?'

Both men nodded, the affirmation leaving a bitter taste in their mouths. 'I swear,' they said in unison.

Gianni raised his hand in blessing. 'Then rise as guards of the Order. From this day on, your lives are not your own. You belong to the Order, to the secret it keeps. And remember this: question nothing. Speak of nothing. Doubt... nothing.'

The words settled over them like a shroud. Paolo swallowed hard, and Francesco reached out to steady him, feeling the slight tremor in his arm. Neither man spoke. They just followed Gianni through twisting hallways, deeper underground, until the grandeur of the Vatican was replaced by stark stone walls and lightless passageways.

'Where are we going?' Paolo whispered, his voice tight with fear.

Francesco shook his head, keeping his gaze forward. He didn't know. And part of him didn't want to.

The air grew colder as they descended, and with each step, the atmosphere grew heavier, pressing in on them like an unseen weight. Finally, they reached a door—an iron door covered in symbols neither of them recognised, sealed with heavy chains that seemed to vibrate with unnatural energy.

'This is your charge,' Gianni said. 'What is behind this door is not just any threat. It is the Church's greatest danger, a being so profound that even speaking of him would condemn you to death. Do not pity him. Do not listen to him. And whatever doubts plague you, you will keep him contained.'

In the flickering candlelight, their white robes brushed against the cold stone floor, the air heavy with the scent of incense and the deeper, earthy odour of ancient, damp stone. Francesco stood tense, his eyes locked on the iron door—the door that led to the secret chamber where the Church's darkest truth was kept. The one they were sworn to guard with their lives. He could feel the pulse, deep and unrelenting, coming from the other side. It was like a heartbeat, rhythmic and sinister, thrumming in time with his own. He swallowed his dread but felt the cold sweat beading on his neck.

Yet it wasn't just a pulse—it felt like a shiver in the walls, a creeping sensation that crawled across the skin. And when Francesco squinted at the symbols on the iron door, he could almost swear they shifted in the candlelight as if they were trying to break free from the metal. It left an impression that something alive—and very old—coiled around the chamber, tightening its grip. But he believed it was the prisoner's doing.

The chamber was suffocating in its stillness. The air felt ancient, heavy with secrets older than the stones themselves. Dim candlelight flickered against the carved sigils etched into the walls, their looping shapes twisting in ways the eye couldn't quite follow. Paolo stood beside Francesco, their robes still crisp and uncreased from the ceremony that had just bound them to the Order of the Hidden Cross.

Neither of them spoke. The silence wasn't just quiet—it was oppressive, sacred in a way neither of them could describe. Paolo's breath was slow, deliberate, as if he were afraid to disturb something lurking in the shadows. Francesco's eyes darted across the room, flickering from symbol to symbol, as though searching for some hidden pattern or answer in their shapes.

Both men felt it—the weight, the watchfulness of something unseen. The purpose of the chamber, the thing they were now sworn to guard, pulsed faintly at the edges of their senses. Whatever it was, it was awake.

Months had passed since that day, though neither Paolo nor Francesco could say exactly how long. Time didn't behave normally in the chamber—it folded, stretched, and frayed at the edges until days bled into nights and back again. They had fallen into a routine, if one could call it that—prayers whispered in tones barely above silence, rituals performed with trembling hands, and long hours spent staring into the middle distance, listening for something they couldn't quite name.

Paolo's once-clean robe was stained now, its edges worn and frayed. Francesco had grown thinner, his sharp cheekbones casting shadows of their own in the dim light. The solemnity of their duty had become a leaden chain around both their necks, dragging them down inch by inch.

Paolo shifted beside Francesco, restless. He felt it too. They both did, though neither had spoken about it. Not until now. The silence pressed down on them, thick and unyielding, making the air feel like water in their lungs.

'You feel it, don't you?' Paolo's voice broke the stillness, low and sharp, slicing through the oppressive quiet. His arms were wrapped tightly across his chest as if he could shield himself from the chill that had settled in his bones, though the chamber was far from cold.

Francesco didn't answer right away. He just stared into the centre of the chamber—the place they had been told never to look for too long, lest it look back. When he finally spoke, his voice was a rasp, thin and cracked from too many sleepless nights.

'Every day, Paolo. I feel it every day.'

The words hung between them, fragile and trembling, like glass suspended by a thread. And for the first time since their initiation, Paolo realised they weren't just guarding something—they were trapped with it.

Paolo's gaze locked on the iron door, his unease written in every crease of his brow. 'He's pushing again, isn't he? Trying to reach us.' His voice trembled, each word heavy with dread, and his eyes flicked to the shadows as though they might rise and swallow him whole.

Francesco let out a slow, controlled breath, trying to regain composure. 'He's always trying,' he replied, voice tight. 'The drugs— they're not enough. Not anymore.'

Paolo hesitated. 'Then why don't we report it? Tell the Order that something's wrong?'

Francesco turned sharply. 'You know why,' he hissed. 'We swore an oath to the Order of the Hidden Cross. We guard this secret with our lives, no matter what. Do you want them to come for us? For you?'

Paolo's lips tightened, but he didn't back down. 'But what if they lied to us?' he whispered, voice trembling. 'What if he's not what they say? What if we've been guarding something—someone—

else?' He lowered his voice further, almost as if speaking to the darkness itself. 'Sometimes, I swear I hear... words. Not whispers—more like... cries. But not in any language I've heard.'

Francesco felt a cold knot in his stomach. He buried these same thoughts deep, too afraid to voice them. But something about the symbols on the door made him uneasy—something in the way they pulsed, like veins carrying some dark energy. Still, he believed that it was the prisoner creating this terror. 'He is what they say he is,' Francesco insisted, voice low and firm, though a slight waver betrayed his doubt. 'A danger to everything. To the Church. To the world.' But even as he spoke, the pulse seemed to grow louder, insistent. It felt like something clawing, begging to be freed—but was it a plea for freedom or a demand from the dark incantations themselves?

Paolo's brow furrowed deeper. 'But what if they were wrong?'

Francesco swallowed, his mouth dry. 'We're not wrong,' he replied, though the words felt hollow. 'He's been in there for thousands of years. If he weren't dangerous, they wouldn't have kept him locked up all this time.'

'I've had dreams,' Paolo confessed quietly. 'Dreams about him.'

Francesco's heart skipped a beat. He'd had the dreams too. Forbidden dreams. The Order demanded silence—about everything. But the dreams were growing stronger. A voice, like a mournful sigh, echoed through the stone halls. A voice pleading for release.

'What dreams?' Francesco asked, his voice barely above a whisper. He wondered if the incantations around the iron door were the source of those dreams, warping their minds to believe the prisoner's intentions were sinister.

'He's calling to me. Like he's in pain. And he's asking me to find someone,' Paolo's voice trembled. 'He keeps saying the same name... "Look for Father Filadelfo." But I don't know why. I just know he's trapped. And I'm the one holding the chains.'

Francesco felt a chill crawl up his spine. He'd heard that name too. The name haunted the edges of his consciousness like a ghost. 'It's the drugs,' Francesco whispered, more to himself than to Paolo. 'We've been down here too long. It messes with your head.'

Paolo shook his head, his face pale. 'What if it's not the drugs? What if he's not supposed to be sedated? What if we're keeping him from... what he's meant to do?'
'Enough!'

Francesco snapped, voice too loud in the oppressive space. 'Do you want to disappear like the others? Do you want to be erased because you're asking too many questions?'

Paolo flinched but didn't look away. 'I know what I'm risking by asking, but it doesn't change what I've seen. What I've felt.' His voice trembled. 'I've seen him, Francesco. He's not a monster. He's broken. And he's trying to reach us.'

Francesco's heart pounded harder, his skin clammy with sweat. He could feel it too—the pull, that faint connection. But was it to the prisoner... or to the dark spells that imprisoned him? The pulse behind the door grew louder, like a heartbeat in the silence, slow and deliberate.

And then it happened.

An alarm—shrill, piercing—echoed through the stone corridors. Francesco's heart stopped. A loud, mechanical whirring filled the chamber, the flickering lights dimming to a dull red.

'No...' Paolo whispered, eyes wide with terror. 'No, not again.'

The air vents hissed, releasing a thin mist that began to creep into the room, pouring into the chamber beyond the iron door. A potent sedative designed to force the figure into submission.

Francesco stood frozen, blood running cold as the alarms blared. He heard movement—something thrashing behind the door, sending chills down his spine. The shadows seemed to dance with the noise, but whether they were a sign of the prisoner's struggle or the enchantments themselves, Francesco could no longer tell.

And then—silence.

The thrashing stopped. The air went still. The alarms faded, but the hiss of gas lingered, seeping into every corner of the chamber. For a moment, Francesco thought he heard something behind the door—a faint, guttural cry that froze his blood—before silence fell like a crushing weight.

'He's sedated,' Francesco whispered, though he didn't know if he was reassuring Paolo or himself. 'He's back under.'

Paolo stood beside him, shaking, drenched in sweat. His eyes were distant, staring through the iron door, lost in the darkness beyond. 'For now,' he muttered. 'But it's only a matter of time.'

Francesco stared at the door, his hands trembling beneath his robe, but then his gaze shifted to Paolo, who still stood rooted to the spot, his face pale and drawn. It wasn't the first time Paolo had spoken out, voiced questions he shouldn't, doubted what should never be doubted. But tonight, there was something different in his voice—an edge, a resolve. A quiet defiance that hadn't been there before.

And that frightened Francesco far more than the pulse behind the door.

'Whatever you're thinking,' Francesco said slowly, his voice barely above a whisper, 'forget it. Don't do anything... stupid.'

Paolo's eyes flickered toward him, but he said nothing. He just stared back at the iron door, his jaw clenched tight, his breath coming out in shallow gasps. Francesco could almost see the thoughts turning behind his eyes—the questions, the fears, and the burning, reckless urge to pull back the veil. To understand what the Order had hidden for so long.

A dangerous urge. A fatal one.

'Promise me,' Francesco pressed, stepping closer, his voice urgent. 'Swear to me you won't say a word about this. To anyone. You know what they do to those who... talk.'

Paolo's expression hardened, and for a moment, Francesco thought he would argue and lash out. But instead, Paolo merely nodded, his face blank, a mask of forced calm. 'I won't talk,' he said quietly. But the words felt hollow, like they had already fallen away into a lie, and Francesco knew, deep down, that this was only the beginning.

A feeling settled in Francesco's gut—a heavy, suffocating certainty that Paolo would not let it go. He could see it in the way Paolo's hands clenched and unclenched at his sides, in the restless flicker of his eyes. A man on the edge of a decision that could not be undone. A man teetering between silence and rebellion.

And for a brief, terrible moment, Francesco thought he saw a shadow shift—not on the iron door but on Paolo himself, like a warning. As if the darkness had reached out to claim him already, whispering his fate.

Francesco turned away, staring back at the iron door. The pulse had stopped, but it would start again. It always did. And the next time, the spells might not hold.

Beside him, Paolo remained silent, still staring into the shadows, where secrets lurked and dreams twisted into nightmares. But Francesco knew the silence would not last. He could already feel Paolo's resolve hardening, his questions taking root in the darkness.

And somewhere deep within, Francesco felt an ache—a mournful certainty that the next pulse, when it came, would not just shake the chamber but tear them apart. That one of them would break, and only one would be left standing.

It was only a matter of time. And time, it seemed, was running out.

Chapter 13

Beris & the Shaman

Beris darted along the forest floor, his tiny feet barely making a sound as he rifled through leaves, twigs, and discarded stones. Every once in a while, he paused, lifting a particularly shiny pebble to the sunlight streaming through the trees. It shimmered, a brilliant sapphire hue. Beris' eyes widened with glee, his fingers tracing its edges.

'Shiny, shiny, shiny,' he whispered, his voice tinged with childlike glee before slipping it into the endless pouch at his side, which seemed to defy any rules of capacity. As soon as the stone disappeared into the endless pocket, his eyes darted elsewhere.

'Squirrel!' Beris shouted, then giggled, distracted by movement.

He moved with a speed and eagerness that belied his size, picking up anything that caught his attention, examining it, and tossing it aside if it failed to hold his interest. A glint of something in the grass caught his eye, but before he could pounce on it, the earth rumbled beneath his feet, causing him to stumble.

'What... what is that?' Beris muttered to himself, his eyes scanning the horizon.

The ground trembled again, but this time, it wasn't just the earth. The rumble grew louder, like thunder rolling through the trees. He spun around just in time to see a cart thundering down the narrow forest path, moving impossibly fast.

Beris ducked behind a tree stump, barely avoiding being trampled by the horses as the cart raced past. The driver, a wild-eyed shaman, screamed at the horses, urging them faster. The cart was piled high with strange objects: masks, wooden totems, and trinkets that clinked and rattled with each bounce. But what truly caught Beris' eye was something gleaming from the back—a glimmering object that shone brighter than the sun itself.

A cat, curled up in the warmth of the sun, lounged lazily on the cart's roof, completely indifferent to the chaos around it. As the cart sped past, Beris' gaze locked onto the shiny object in the back.

Without a second thought, he darted out from his hiding spot, the thundering hooves of the horses echoing in his ears. His heart raced as his eyes locked onto the glimmering object in the back of the cart, a gleaming jewel nestled among trinkets and oddities.

'I need that. I need it.' As he breathed out, his voice trembling with desire.

The shine of it tugged at his very soul, a magnet for his insatiable hunger for all things precious. It called to him, a light in the chaos of the forest, and Beris, small as he was, could not resist.

He scanned his surroundings frantically, searching for a way to chase after the fast-moving cart. That's when he saw it—a rabbit, no more than a few feet away, munching contentedly on a patch of clover. Without hesitation, Beris' eyes narrowed, and with a flick of his thoughts, the rabbit's movements froze. The creature's eyes glazed over, falling under the enchantment of Beris' control. With a swift hop, Beris mounted the rabbit, his tiny hands gripping its fur.

'Go!' he commanded, his voice sharp with urgency.

The rabbit leapt forward, its strong legs pushing off the ground with surprising speed. The forest blurred around them as they darted between the trees, leaves rustling and twigs snapping underfoot. But it didn't take long for Beris to realise that the rabbit, despite its best efforts, was no match for the horses. The gap between them and the cart was widening, the gleam of the treasure growing smaller by the second.

'Not fast enough!' Beris cursed under his breath, his heart pounding in frustration.

The rabbit was swift, but the cart's wild speed left it behind. Frustration gnawed at Beris as the shimmering treasure slipped further from view.

He didn't have time to waste. He had to switch. His eyes darted through the underbrush until they landed on a fox, its sharp eyes catching the gleam of daylight as it slunk between the trees. Perfect.

With a flicker of thought, Beris released the rabbit from his control and turned his focus to the fox. The creature halted mid-step, its instincts overridden by Beris' will. Without missing a beat, Beris leapt from the rabbit onto the fox's back, the animal immediately responding to the new connection.

'Run!' Beris hissed, his voice tense with urgency.

The fox shot forward, its lithe body weaving through the thick undergrowth with ease. Beris clung tightly to its fur as they sped through the trees, the wind whipping against his face. The ground seemed to vanish beneath them as the fox leapt over fallen branches and dodged between tree trunks. For a moment, Beris felt a surge of hope—the fox was faster, more agile, and they were closing the gap.

But the horses were too far ahead, their powerful strides devouring the distance between them and the fading cart. The rumbling of the wheels over the uneven forest path sent a cloud of dust into the air, making it harder for Beris to keep his eyes on the prize. He ground his teeth in frustration, knowing the fox couldn't keep up.

'No, no, no!' he muttered through gritted teeth. His mind raced, searching for another option. The gleaming object in the cart seemed to taunt him, growing fainter by the moment, slipping through his grasp.

Then, his eyes caught sight of a bird—a crow—perched on a low-hanging branch. Its small, beady eyes blinked lazily as it preened its feathers, completely unaware of the frantic chase unfolding below. Beris didn't hesitate. He knew what he had to do.

With another flick of his thoughts, the connection with the fox snapped, and the crow's mind was instantly consumed by Beris' control. The bird flapped its wings, confused at first, but Beris' will was too strong. He leapt from the fox's back just as it skidded to a halt, his small form light as a feather as he grasped onto the crow's back.

'Up!' he commanded, his voice barely a whisper but full of command.

The crow took flight, its wings beating furiously as it lifted Beris into the air. The forest floor shrank beneath him, the trees turning into a sea of green. The cart, now far ahead, rumbled down the path, but from his new vantage point, Beris could see everything clearly.

The wind howled in his ears as the bird soared higher, and for a moment, Beris forgot the chase. The world below him was vast and wild, stretching out in every direction. The sun bathed the treetops in golden light, and the forest seemed to breathe, alive with the hum of nature. But Beris shook his head, forcing himself to focus. There would be time to admire the beauty of the world later. Right now, all that mattered was the shining treasure in the back of that cart.

He directed the crow to circle above the cart, watching it from high above. The horses galloped relentlessly, their hooves kicking up dirt and leaves as they tore through the forest. The shaman, still shouting at them to go faster, seemed oblivious to the small figure gliding overhead.

Beris' eyes gleamed as he assessed his next move. The cart bounced violently over the uneven ground, but Beris could see a moment, a single opportunity. As the cart hit a large rock, the back corner lifted slightly, jostling the items in the rear. Now. This was his chance.

With a burst of speed, the crow dove, plummeting through the air like a stone. The world blurred around Beris as they streaked toward the cart. Timing was everything. The crow's wings folded tightly, its beak pointed like an arrowhead. The wind roared in Beris' ears, but he focused on the shimmering object.

Just as the crow neared the cart, Beris jumped, his tiny form landing in the back with a soft thud. His heart raced, his breath coming in quick bursts as he scrambled for cover, hiding behind a bag of grain. The crow flew off, free from Beris' control, leaving him alone with his prize.

He peeked out from behind the bag, scanning his surroundings. The cat, who had been sleeping on top of the cart, stirred slightly, its ears twitching as if sensing something. Beris held his breath, watching the feline closely. But after a moment, the cat stretched, yawned, and settled back into its sun-soaked nap.

Relief washed over Beris, though his heart still pounded in his chest. The cart bounced and rattled beneath him, the horses' hooves thudding in his ears. But now, he was closer. Closer to the shimmering treasure that had caught his eye.

It was there, just within reach.

Suddenly, the cart took a sharp turn off the path, entering a large clearing in the forest's heart. Beris peered out from his hiding spot just in time to see the horses come to a grinding halt. The shaman jumped down from his seat and walked to the centre of the clearing, his eyes scanning the space with a look of purpose.

Beris, still hiding behind the sack, watched as the shaman raised his hands toward the sky, muttering something in a language Beris had never heard before. The air grew thick, and without warning, every item in the back of the cart began to rise. Beris' eyes widened in awe and fear. Trinkets, tools, and treasures spun like leaves caught in a whirlwind. There was no wind, no force of nature behind this phenomenon—only the will of the shaman's chant.

He ducked down lower, hiding himself from the view of the cat, which still slept through the chaos. The items began to spin faster and faster, whirling into a chaotic spiral. The very earth trembled as trees groaned, roots ripping from the soil, and plants, rocks, and pieces of the forest floor began converging into the whirlwind.

Beris gasped as a massive swirl of debris surrounded him. He tried to hold on to the cart's edge, but the force was too great. Without thinking, he jumped from the cart, landing awkwardly beside the wheel just as the shaman lowered his hands.

And then, as if the very world itself held its breath, everything stopped.

The chaotic whirlwind collapsed in on itself, spiralling inward with a velocity that defied reason. Trees, branches, leaves, and fragments of earth twisted together in a violent dance, their forms blurring into a single chaotic mass. The very air seemed to crackle with energy, charged with an ancient power that hummed in the bones of the forest. Birds scattered from the treetops, their cries drowned out by the furious gusts of wind that whipped through the clearing. Even the sky seemed to bow under the weight of it, darkening as if it too were being drawn into the vortex.

For a fleeting moment, just as the chaos reached its zenith, the world seemed to hold its breath. The swirling debris, the storm of matter, halted mid-air, suspended by some unseen force. Time stretched out impossibly thin, as though the entire forest were balancing on the edge of a knife. In that stillness, the roar of the storm became a deafening silence, the kind of silence that makes the heart stop for fear that any sound could shatter the fragile illusion of peace.

Then, with a soundless snap, it happened.

Everything—the swirling branches, the twisting shards of earth, the disjointed pieces of the world—converged into a single point. The convergence was so absolute, so precise, that it was as though the universe itself had been folded down to a singularity. For the briefest of moments, it was as if reality itself blinked, caught between two breaths.

And then, just as suddenly, the chaos was gone.

In its place, standing as though it had always been there, was a cottage. It was a modest thing, yet it radiated an inexplicable sense of permanence as though it had existed for centuries, tucked away in the forgotten corners of the world. Weathered stone walls, covered in patches of moss, stood firm and unyielding. The wooden shingles on the roof, dulled by time, sloped gently, and a thin plume of smoke curled lazily from the chimney as though a fire had been burning for hours. Flowerpots, filled with bright blooms that should not have survived the vortex, lined the windowsills, and a cobbled path led to a sturdy oak door, its handle gleaming faintly in the fading light.

The air in the clearing was still now, almost unnaturally so. The chaotic storm that had ravaged the forest moments before had left no trace of its violence. The trees stood untouched, their branches swaying gently in a breeze that no longer carried the weight of ancient magic. The only sound was the soft crackling of the fire inside the cottage, welcoming the return of peace.

It was as though the cottage had not been built but had simply become—willed into existence by forces beyond comprehension. A structure born not of wood and stone but of raw magic and the will of the shaman who now stood in its shadow, surveying his creation with an air of quiet satisfaction.

The shaman, his gnarled hands still raised from the final gesture of his spell, lowered them slowly, his breath coming in slow, deliberate exhales. His face, lined with age and wisdom, betrayed no surprise at the sight before him. This was no accident. This was the culmination of a ritual older than memory, a magic woven through time itself. He had called forth this cottage from the chaos, from the very bones of the earth, and it had answered. It stood now, as timeless and enduring as the forest that surrounded it.

Yet, for all its apparent serenity, there was something unsettling about the cottage. Something that spoke of ancient secrets buried deep within its walls. Something that hinted at a power far greater than the stones and mortar that made up its form.

But for now, in this moment, it simply stood. Timeless.

Beris stared wide-eyed as the shaman walked over to the horses, unhitching them and guiding them to a stable that had not existed a moment ago. The shaman muttered soothing words to the animals, feeding them hay as though this were the most ordinary thing in the world.

Beris, still trembling, took the opportunity to slip inside the cottage. If the outside was magical, the inside was downright mystical. A teapot floated across the room, pouring itself into a cup that rested in mid-air. The shaman sat in a chair, picking up a book and sipping the tea without so much as a glance at the floating objects.

The cup hovered in the air, waiting for the next sip.

Beris took the opportunity now that the cat was asleep and the shaman had drifted into a light slumber, the book resting lazily in his
hands. The soft crackling of the fire and the rhythmic sound of the
shaman's slow breaths created a gentle lull that filled the room.
This was his chance to explore without being noticed, to uncover
the secrets of this strange, magical cottage and—most important-
ly—to find the shiny object that had caught his eye in the back of
the cart.

He tiptoed quietly into the open, every instinct telling him to move
with care. The room was alive with magic, each corner infused with
an unseen energy that made the very air hum. But it was the kitchen
that truly held his attention. Beris' eyes widened as he stepped closer,
drawn in by an almost hypnotic scene playing out before him.

A knife hovered in mid-air, spinning effortlessly as it sliced through
vegetables on the kitchen counter. Potatoes, onions, carrots—all were
chopped with precision, their pieces landing neatly in a bubbling pot
suspended over the fire. The soft hissing and bubbling sounds of the
stew filled the room, and a mouth-watering aroma wafted up, causing
Beris' stomach to rumble in spite of himself.

The knife worked quickly and with purpose, moving from vegetable
to vegetable without hesitation, as if guided by an invisible hand.
It was not alone. Around it, other objects floated lazily in the air—
spoons stirring the pot, herbs being plucked from bunches hanging
above, and even a cloth wiping up the occasional splash. All of it was
carried out with the same silent precision, as if orchestrated by some
unseen chef who had no need for physical form.

Beris stood there for a moment in awe, watching the cooking scene
unfold before him. It was mesmerising. The stew simmered with a
low, contented burble, and every now and then, a ladle would rise
from the countertop, dip into the pot, and pour a taste into a floating
bowl as though sampling its own work. The smell was intoxicating,
a rich blend of herbs and vegetables that filled the air with warmth
and comfort.

But Beris, despite being thoroughly entranced, shook his head after a few long moments to come back to the reality of his mission. He was here for something much shinier than a stew — he couldn't lose focus now.

As his eyes roved across the room, he finally spotted it. Tucked under the window, hidden in the shadows but unmistakable in its allure, was a box. More like a chest, its wooden frame was etched with delicate carvings, and even from this distance, Beris could tell it was something special. His heart quickened with excitement. This had to be it. This was where the real treasure was kept.

Carefully, Beris crept toward the chest, mindful not to disturb the floating objects still busy at work. His small hands hovered over the lock, and with a deft twist of his fingers, the latch clicked open.

The lid creaked slightly as Beris slowly lifted it, revealing a sight that made his breath catch in his throat. Inside, gleaming in the dim light, was a fortune — diamonds, rubies, sapphires, and gold glittered before him, each jewel more stunning than the last. It was as though the stars themselves had been captured and stored away in this small chest.

For a moment, Beris could hardly contain his excitement. He had never seen so many beautiful, shimmering things in one place. He began stuffing his pouch with the most dazzling gems, his tiny hands moving quickly as if the treasure might vanish at any moment.

But before he could get far, something shifted in the room. There was a sudden weight in the air, and Beris froze, a shiver running down his spine. An invisible force gripped him, pulling him away from the chest and lifting him into the air. His heart pounded in his chest as he struggled, but it was no use — he was caught.

Slowly, a faint shimmer revealed the outline of a figure — a servant, invisible until now, held Beris aloft. The creature's form flickered as it moved, as if light bent around its being, and without a word, it whisked Beris over to the shaman, who still sat in his chair, now stirring slightly as he drifted between sleep and wakefulness.

With a firm nudge, the invisible servant kicked the shaman awake, thrusting Beris into his view.

The shaman stirred groggily, blinking in confusion. His eyes, heavy with sleep, focused on the small creature dangling in mid-air. Slowly, the shaman's confusion gave way to understanding, and a bemused smile tugged at the corner of his mouth.

With a flick of his wrist, the shaman made a simple gesture. Beris' pouch floated over, spilling its contents into the shaman's outstretched palms. The gems poured out in a stream, more than the shaman could hold, overflowing and spilling onto the floor in a cascade of glittering wealth.

Beris stared in horror, his small body trembling as he floated helplessly. The shaman's eyes, a mix of disappointment and amusement, shifted to the sleeping cat. With a click of his tongue, he gave the cat a disapproving look.

'You should have been watching him,' the shaman muttered to the cat, who merely blinked sleepily before stretching out again, unbothered.

The shaman turned back to Beris, his expression softening. 'You little thief,' he murmured, almost kindly.

But his hand moved with purpose. A glass cube materialised around Beris, trapping him in an invisible prison. Beris pressed his tiny hands against the walls, bewildered. He could see through it, but there was no escape.

As Beris floated helplessly in the grip of the invisible servant, panic seized him. His tiny heart pounded in his chest, the shimmering treasure he had so greedily taken now scattered across the floor, the weight of his situation closing in like the walls of a cage. Desperation clawed at his thoughts, and with a wild flicker of hope, he remembered the memory-erasing chants he had learned long ago.

If he could just make the shaman forget... forget that he ever saw him... forget he existed at all... then he could escape this nightmare.

'Vella'tir som'nara!' he shouted, the words slipping from his tongue in a frantic, hurried chant. His small voice, shrill and trembling, filled the room as he cast the spell in a last-ditch attempt to salvage his freedom. 'Mellis'caro dormas vi'nara!'

But the shaman barely blinked. His eyes were on the floating jewels, the stream of treasure pouring from Beris' pouch into his out-stretched hands, as if nothing more than a passing curiosity.

Beris' voice cracked, his chants growing more frenzied. 'Diss'tara! Mela'tris fortas!' The ancient words tumbled out of him, each one more desperate than the last, his hands flailing against the invisible prison that held him in mid-air. 'Forga'rem, forget!' he screamed, the final plea leaving his throat raw.

But the shaman paid no attention to the foibles of this little creature. His focus didn't waver. He barely even glanced up, his expression calm and almost amused as Beris' magic sputtered into the air and dissolved like mist. To the shaman, these weak little spells were nothing—fleeting wisps of nonsense that couldn't even scratch the surface of his ancient knowledge.

Beris' voice faltered, the last of his chants falling silent in the thick air. He watched in helpless disbelief as his memory spells had no effect, not even a flicker of recognition from the shaman. The power imbalance was overwhelming. His magic was nothing here, just the impotent cry of a creature far too small for the world he'd tried to steal from.

The shaman let the last of the gems trickle through his fingers, his gaze settling on Beris with a quiet, measured intensity.

And in that moment, Beris realised there was no escape. He whispered the words like a lullaby, clinging to the hope they'd work this time.

The shaman stood, walking to a bookshelf. He thumbed through a few old tomes, muttering to himself. After finding the right one, he nodded, satisfied, and walked back to Beris. He opened the book, his finger tracing the ancient text as he read the words aloud.

Beris felt the world shift around him. The air grew cold, and a darkness thicker than any night pressed in from all sides. His body felt weightless, suspended in a void that defied description.

The light of the cottage dimmed, growing distant as the shaman's voice became a murmur in the background. Beris' heart raced as his world began to dissolve into nothingness. The familiar objects of the cottage—the floating tea, the knife chopping vegetables, the simmering stew—faded from view, replaced by an all-encompassing blackness.

And then, with a final, wrenching pull, Beris was cast into the Dark Matter.

There was no light here. No sound. The world he had known moments ago dissolved into an inky void, and with it went any sense of orientation. He couldn't tell if his eyes were open or closed. He couldn't feel his hands, his legs, or even the air on his skin. It was as if his very existence was being erased, bit by bit.

'P-please,' he whispered, his voice swallowed by the endless void. No echo. No response.

Panic gripped him. He tried to scream, but the sound died in his throat, muted by the oppressive silence. His heart raced, but even that, he could not hear. Time had no meaning in this place. Seconds stretched into eternity, and Beris, once so full of life and energy, was reduced to a drifting speck in an ocean of nothingness.

He drifted, weightless and voiceless, a speck consumed by infinite emptiness. The vast void pressed against him, smothering even his memories. For the first time, Beris understood the true meaning of loneliness—not absence, but the crushing presence of nothingness.

Tears welled in his eyes, though he could not feel them fall. In this vast, empty darkness, he realised what he had truly lost. Not the shiny gems or treasures, but the warmth of the world, the feel of the earth beneath his feet, the sound of the wind in the trees. It was all gone, and in its place was this infinite, cold void.

He had chased after something shiny, only to find himself lost in the dark.

The shaman, satisfied, closed the book and returned to his chair.

For a brief moment, as the book settled on his lap, a faint shadow of something akin to sorrow flickered across the shaman's weathered face. His gaze lingered on the empty space where Beris had once been, now just a faint memory in the quiet cottage. The flicker of amusement and bemusement that had lit his eyes before had dimmed, replaced by something older, heavier.

As he leaned back in his chair, his thoughts drifted to another time, to another mischievous spirit. An old friend—long gone now— who had once roamed these woods with the same playful recklessness. He remembered the laughter that echoed through the trees, the trickery that always came with a smile, and the mischief that had been harmless—mostly. They had stolen time together, in those days, chasing the shimmer of life's fleeting joys.

A nostalgic ache bloomed quietly in the back of his mind, soft but persistent. That friend, drawn to the same glittering distractions, had vanished long ago—swallowed by the very magic they once delighted in. For a moment, Beris' small form was a reflection of that lost companion, a fleeting spark doomed to flicker out. Perhaps it was the nature of small, bright souls to chase after what dazzled until they found themselves caught in the dark.

The shaman blinked, the weight of years settling on his shoulders. He hadn't thought about that old companion in centuries, and the memory was bittersweet—sharp in its clarity, dulled by the passing of too many years. For just a moment, Beris' fate had stirred something deep within him—a recognition of what the little creature had been searching for.

But time moves on, he reminded himself. And those who chase what glitters too eagerly often fall into their own shadows.

He sighed deeply, shaking the nostalgia from his bones. With a final glance at the place where Beris had been, he let the memory slip from his thoughts, like a leaf drifting downriver. His eyes grew heavy, his mind clouded with sleep.

The cat stirred by the fire, purring softly as the crackling flames cast flickering shadows on the walls. The invisible servant, ever-watchful, lingered in the corner, waiting for the next command. The shaman, lost in the haze of old memories and fading thoughts, drifted off into a quiet slumber, the weight of the years cradling him into sleep.

The cottage, once full of light and life, felt somehow emptier now.

Beris reached out, but his hands met nothing. The emptiness pressed in, cold and infinite, stealing even his tears before they could fall, not from fear, but from a profound, hollow loneliness. His world had been reduced to shadows and silence, and he realised In the darkness, Beris thought not of the gems but of the forest—the rustling leaves, the warmth of sunlight. He reached for it, but it was gone, leaving only the shadows he had chased.

He was just Beris—small, alone, and utterly forsaken.

Chapter 14

The Erased

Paulo sat in his cold, stone chamber, the flame of his oil lamp flickering weakly against the oppressive darkness. His hand trembled as it gripped a quill, hovering above the parchment. The air was thick with must and the scent of ink, but beneath that, a deeper, darker presence loomed—something Paulo couldn't shake since the moment he laid eyes on Him.

The Order demanded silence. Every guard was sworn to an oath from the moment they were tapped on the shoulder—a weight Paulo had carried without question until the whispers began. Until tonight.

His eyes drifted to the door, still shut, still locked, but offering little reassurance. The events of the night replayed in his mind, over and over, like a haunting refrain. The chamber below the monastery—the forbidden place far beneath the Vatican—where he had been sent on a simple errand. A task meant to be quick and uneventful.

But instead, he had seen Him. Yehoshua.

No, not the Yehoshua he had learned of in scripture. Not the glorious, ascended figure that had risen to the right hand of God. This was something far more terrible, something more grotesque. This was a man—barely a man—dangling between life and death, held in a perpetual state of suffering by powers Paulo could barely comprehend.

Yehoshua's body had been mutilated by time, decayed but unyielding to death. His skin hung like thin parchment over brittle bones, pocked with ancient, festering wounds. They had never healed. They couldn't. His eyes—sunken, hollow—had twitched as Paulo entered the chamber, his lids fluttering as if trying to open. There had been no divine light in those eyes. Only suffering.

Paulo heard the faintest sound from Yehoshua's lips—like a groan, like a man trying to speak after centuries of silence. It was a sound that would haunt Paulo for the rest of his short life.

'Paulo,' came the weak, rasping voice.

Paulo's breath caught in his throat, and he stepped closer, almost against his will. His heart pounded in his chest as the broken figure on the stone slab struggled to raise his head. Then, with the effort of a man pushing through an eternity of pain, the man whispered, 'I am Yehoshua.'

The words were barely audible, as though they had taken every ounce of strength the ancient figure had left. His body trembled slightly, as if even speaking those words had drained what little life remained in him. Paulo's blood turned cold. This was Yehoshua?—the Yehoshua? His mind screamed in protest, refusing to accept the truth that lay before him. Everything he had been taught, everything he had believed—it was all unravelling in this single, horrifying moment. He knew there was a truth to these words, he just knew it.

He stumbled backwards, nearly tripping over his feet as he tried to comprehend what he had just heard. This was not supposed to be possible. Yehoshua had ascended—he had risen—yet, here he was, broken and barely alive, in a hidden chamber beneath the monastery. Could this broken, suffering creature truly be the Messiah? Paulo's mind reeled at the thought—his years of prayer and devotion seemed to mock him now, a cruel echo against the grotesque reality before him. And now that truth, or whatever it was, lay festering in a hidden chamber beneath the monastery, forgotten and broken.

Panic gripped Paulo, tightening around his chest like a vice. He couldn't stay here. He couldn't bear to be in the presence of this... this thing that should not be. His legs moved before his mind could catch up, and he fled the room, locking it in behind him, his footsteps echoing wildly in the narrow corridors as he raced back to his chamber.

Slamming the door shut behind him, Paulo collapsed against the cold stone wall, his heart thundering in his ears. He gasped for breath, his hands trembling uncontrollably. The truth clawed at him, ripping apart everything he thought he knew. Yehoshua had not ascended, had not risen. He had been kept prisoner, trapped in a state between life and death, hidden away from the world.

Paulo's head spun as he fought to process the weight of the revelation. The Order of the Hidden Cross, the very sect he had devoted his life to, was built on a lie. A horrible, insidious lie. The Messiah was not the glorified figure the Church proclaimed. He was a prisoner, broken and reduced to nothing more than a frail shell of his former self.

Paulo's breaths came in ragged gasps as he tried to steady himself. He couldn't let this stay hidden. He had to document what he had seen, what he now knew to be true. But his hands shook so violently that it took several tries to light the small oil lamp on his desk.

He grabbed a scrap of parchment and dipped his quill into the ink, his heart still racing as his thoughts tumbled out in a frenzied scrawl.

'I have seen him. I have seen Yehoshua, alive but barely, hidden in a chamber below the monastery. He is not dead. He has not risen. The Order has lied. Everything is a lie.'

His hand shook, smearing the ink. Paulo paused, his breath shallow and uneven. The enormity of what he was writing felt like a weight on his chest, crushing him with each stroke of the quill. He couldn't believe what he was doing. If anyone found out, if the Order learned of his treachery, he would be silenced—erased, just like the others. But the world had to know.

As he wrote, the temperature in the room began to drop. At first, he thought it was his nerves, the adrenaline finally leaving his body, but then the air grew colder. A thick, oppressive cold that pressed down on him like the weight of a thousand winters. His breath misted in the lamplight, and the shadows around him deepened, growing darker and more tangible.

Paulo froze, his quill still hovering above the parchment.

Something was here.

The temperature dropped suddenly, the chill biting into Paulo's skin. The shadows seemed to twist, curling at the edges, and then... the scratching started, slow at first like something sharp against stone. Paulo's heart skipped a beat as the sound grew closer and louder. He turned his head, his eyes locking on the corner of the room where the demon began to materialise.

The shadows on the walls twisted and contorted, and from the corner of the chamber, a shape began to emerge. It was darker than the night itself, a figure that seemed to swallow the light around it. And then he saw it.

Paulo stared at the demon, heart pounding in his chest, eyes wide in terror. The room had grown impossibly cold, and every shadow seemed alive, pulsing with some ancient malevolence that made the very air feel toxic. He couldn't move—his legs were like stone, rooted to the spot by the horror of what stood before him.

The demon was a thing of nightmares. Its hulking form twisted between flesh and shadow, its skin slick and oily, like the darkest part of a forgotten abyss. Its eyes glowed a deep, violent red, flickering with an unnatural hunger. It wasn't just a physical presence—it was something deeper, something far more ancient than anything Paulo had ever imagined. The creature seemed to radiate darkness itself, a force of primordial evil that devoured everything around it, leaving only the cold, empty air of despair in its wake.

'You know too much,' the demon hissed, its voice slithering through the air like smoke. 'Now, you must be taken.'

Paulo's breath caught in his throat as the demon raised one clawed hand, fingers longer than his forearm and ending in wickedly sharp points. His legs screamed to run, but they refused to move. His heart hammered against his ribs as if it could escape the fate his body was already succumbing to. He opened his mouth to scream, to plead, but his voice was stolen by the crushing terror that held him in place.

The demon stepped closer, its claws dripping with shadows that slithered along the stone floor. Paulo felt a wave of nausea as the creature reached toward him, its sharp, black talons hovering over his chest. For a brief moment, there was a pause, as though time itself had frozen. Then, with a swift, sickening motion, the demon drove one claw into Paulo's chest.

A wave of pain, sharper than anything Paulo had ever known, exploded through his body. His breath caught in a strangled gasp as the claw pierced his flesh, the sound of tearing skin and muscle filling the chamber. The demon's talon moved slowly, deliberately, as if savouring every moment. Paulo's vision blurred as tears welled up in his eyes, the sheer agony forcing him to his knees.

And then it began.

The claw wasn't just tearing his body—it was opening something inside him, ripping a hole not just in his flesh but in the very fabric of his existence. It was as if the demon's claw was a key, unlocking some hidden, cursed part of him that had always been waiting to be torn open. Paulo felt a pull like an unseen hand was reaching into him, grabbing hold of something deep within his chest and yanking it out.

The demon grinned, a grotesque mockery of satisfaction, as the tear in Paulo's chest grew wider. Not just blood but something darker began to seep out—an inky blackness, as though his very soul was leaking from the wound. The world around him began to warp, twisting and spinning, as if reality itself was breaking apart.

Paulo tried to scream, but no sound came out. His body was no longer his own; it was being devoured by the rift that the demon had carved into him. Slowly, impossibly, he felt himself being pulled into the tear—into the dark opening in his chest. His body jerked violently as it was dragged toward the wound, inch by inch, like a puppet with its strings pulled by some cruel, unseen hand.

He could feel his bones cracking, splintering under the force of whatever lay beyond that tear. His skin stretched and tore, his muscles ripping apart as he was drawn into the abyss. He felt his ribs snap one by one, the pain so intense that he nearly blacked out, but some malevolent force kept him conscious, forced him to experience every moment of his body being torn apart.

His legs, his arms, everything was being pulled into that gaping wound, being absorbed into the darkness. He looked down in horror to see his limbs twisting, folding unnaturally into the black void that the demon had opened within him. It was as though he were collapsing into himself, his body contorting and breaking as it was sucked into the endless dark.

The pain was unbearable, beyond anything a human should have been able to endure. Every nerve in his body was on fire, his skin ripping apart as the darkness consumed him. His bones splintered like dry wood, his muscles tore with wet, sickening snaps, and his very essence was dragged toward the abyss, piece by agonising piece.

As his body broke apart, Paulo's mind began to splinter as well. His thoughts unravelled, scattered in the howling void. He could feel his memories, his identity, everything that made him—him, being ripped away, slipping into the infinite darkness. His whole life, the monastery, the faces of those he cared for and loved—they all flickered and vanished, consumed by the void, leaving only cold, empty silence.

Paulo's consciousness began to slip, fragments of himself breaking away as the void consumed him. But even as his body and soul were being torn apart, he felt something else—the darkness was not empty. It was alive. It was waiting for him.

He felt it, in the endless black. Something ancient. Something watching. And then, suddenly, he was falling. His stomach lurched as the ground disappeared beneath him, and he plunged into the abyss. The darkness rushed up to meet him, swallowing him whole, enveloping him in a cold, suffocating embrace. His limbs flailed uselessly as he tumbled through the void, his screams swallowed by the oppressive silence that surrounded him.

There was no up or down, no direction to orient himself. He was weightless, suspended in the black nothingness that stretched infinitely in all directions. The only sound was the pounding of his heartbeat, deafening in the silence.

And then, it began.

The first tendrils of dark matter reached out to him, slithering over his skin like serpents, cold and unyielding. They coiled around his limbs, tightening their grip, squeezing the life out of him. He struggled, but it was futile. The tendrils were not physical—there was nothing to grab, nothing to fight against. They seeped into his skin, penetrating deeper, wrapping around his bones, his organs, his mind.

He had no time to comprehend the full horror of it before he was pulled further into the void, his body and soul disintegrating into the blackness. Paulo was no more.

In the chamber, the demon stood over the bloodstained stone floor, its eyes flickering with faint, malicious satisfaction. The job was done. The demon retreated back into the shadows.

But it wasn't alone.

A mist stirred in the corner of the room, a figure barely discernible in the dim light of the flickering oil lamps. The memory keeper stepped forward, its pale, featureless face reflecting nothing but cold detachment. It moved with an eerie grace, its presence almost imperceptible yet undeniably powerful.

It approached the desk where Paulo had begun to write his account. The memory keeper gently lifted the parchment from the desk, the report Paulo had been so desperate to complete. It examined the words for a moment, then its hand hovered over the parchment, its translucent fingers tracing the words scrawled in a frantic, desperate hand. The ink on the page began to bleed, the letters dissolving into nothingness as though they had never existed.

As the last word faded from the parchment, the room fell silent, the faint scent of blood still lingering in the air. The Order's secrets remained safe. Paulo was erased, not just from the monastery, but from history itself. No memory of him would survive. No echo of his name would be whispered. It was as if he had never been born.

Yet the memory keeper did not leave.

Its form, spectral and thin, glided across the room toward the wall, pausing at a blank section of stone. With one slender, almost translucent finger, it began to carve a symbol into the wall, its touch leaving faint glowing lines in its wake. The lines twisted and curved, forming a shape that defied logic—a symbol that seemed to pulse with its own life as if it existed in dimensions beyond human comprehension.

The symbol flickered faintly before dimming, its presence etched not just into stone but into the very fabric of the room. It was not a mere mark—it was a seal, binding the room and the Order's secrets in eternal silence.

The memory keeper took one last glance around the room, ensuring that all evidence had been erased, that Paulo's existence had been entirely scrubbed from reality. Satisfied, it turned toward the door, its movements eerily graceful, and vanished into the shadows from whence it came.

But the symbol remained.

Though invisible to most, it was there—a twisted, pulsating mark etched into the fabric of the stone. It wasn't just a symbol. It was a warning. A sign that Paulo's fate had been sealed long before he had stepped into that hidden chamber. A sign that others had come before him. And others would follow.

As the room fell silent once again, a faint gust of wind stirred the dust, revealing that Paulo's name, once scrawled on the wall by some long-forgotten hand, had also disappeared, replaced by a small, barely discernible inscription etched beneath the symbol.

Ego sum ultimus. Non primus. Non solus.

I am the last. Not the first. Not the only one.

The stone walls had seen countless souls vanish within their cold embrace, and this chamber would witness countless more. Paulo was gone. His memory, his body, and his very existence erased. But the cycle was far from over.

The next soul had already been chosen.

Chapter 15

Father Filadelfo

A terrified young girl, no more than eight, burst into the chapel, her small hands trembling as she pulled at Father Filadelfo's robes.

'Father, come quickly!' she gasped, her voice strained with panic.

'What is it, child?' Filadelfo asked, his heart already quickening in response to her urgency.

'He's hurting her. You have to stop him!'

Without waiting for an answer, the girl darted down the hallway. Father Filadelfo sprang up from his meditative posture, the peaceful rhythm of his prayers shattered by the girl's terror. He followed, his feet pounding the stone floors of the monastery, struggling to keep pace with the child as she raced through winding corridors and vaulted halls.

'Who is being hurt?' he called after her, but she didn't respond. The girl's ragged breaths echoed through the empty passages, her pace frantic, driven by a fear too great to explain.

Finally, she stopped by a small window that overlooked the garden. The girl pointed a trembling finger toward the glasshouse.

'There! He's hurting her. She's bleeding, bleeding a lot.'

Father Filadelfo leaned toward the window, squinting. His heart lurched. Through the daylight a brilliant light shone from the glass-house, bright enough to obscure whatever horror was happening inside.

What light could be shining so brightly in the middle of the day? The question clawed at his mind, but he had no time to dwell on it. He had to act.

He rushed down toward the garden, navigating through the winding paths of overgrown hedges and statues of saints. His breath came in shallow bursts as he weaved through low-hanging branches and prickly vines, barely feeling the scratches against his skin. When he finally reached the grand doors of the glasshouse, the priest hes-itated. For a brief moment, dread gripped him—something terrible awaited inside. But his duty as a man of faith pulled him forward.

He drew a deep breath, crossed himself, and flung open the door.

Blinding light met him immediately, forcing him to shield his eyes. He blinked rapidly, trying to make out anything through the intense glow. Faintly, through the brilliance, he heard soft weeping, the unmistakable sound of a child crying.

He quickened his pace, stumbling down the stone path as the bright light disoriented him.

Then, as he rounded the corner, the scene before him froze him in place.

'No... no, it can't be...' Father Filadelfo whispered, horror choking the breath from his lungs.

Before him was the Monsignor—at least, what looked like him—bathed in radiant light, his skin glowing as if illuminated from within. But the act he was engaged in, vile and unspeakable, was far from holy. The man, or creature, had the girl pinned beneath him on a stone bench. The child lay motionless, her small, broken body drenched in blood. And yet, despite the horror of the scene, the thing wearing the Monsignor's face continued, its mouth curling into a wicked grin as its glowing eyes met Father Filadelfo's.

It licked its lips, as if savouring the moment, then glanced at the priest with a sickening look—one that said, You're next.

The creature looked like an angel, but it behaved like a demon.

Father Filadelfo stood paralysed, his mind torn between disbelief and fury. This thing could not be the man he knew—it was something else, something unnatural. A violent surge of righteous anger overtook him.
'In the name of our Lord Jesus Christ, stop!' he shouted, his voice trembling but firm. He lunged toward the creature, his crucifix swinging from his neck as he leapt onto its back.

In his haste, Filadelfo barely noticed the heat radiating from the creature's body. As he grappled with the thing, the silver crucifix around his neck fell against the creature's flesh. The moment the cross touched its skin, the light began to change—flickering and warping as if the creature was unravelling from within.

The creature let out a scream, an inhuman sound that pierced the air. Its spine arched back, its body convulsing violently. Father Filadelfo was thrown off, landing hard on the stone floor. Dazed, he watched in shock as the radiant light that had surrounded the creature was sucked inward, vacuumed into the thing's core until all that remained was the Monsignor, limp and lifeless, slumped over the girl.

The girl, barely conscious, lay beneath him, too weak to push him off. Filadelfo scrambled to his feet, his head spinning with disbelief. He dragged the dead weight of the Monsignor's body off the girl, casting it aside with disgust. He quickly removed his outer robe, covering the child's battered form, shielding her from the horror she had endured.

The young girl who had alerted Filadelfo came running to her friend's side. She knelt beside her, gently stroking the unconscious girl's hair, her tiny body shaking with quiet sobs. Something no child should ever have to witness—yet here she was, offering comfort in the face of unimaginable horror.

Father Filadelfo's mind reeled. His gaze fell to the ground, where blood pooled beneath the girl. There was so much of it. How had this happened? The violence had broken her, far beyond the loss of innocence. It was as though something inside her had been ripped apart. He couldn't tell if the wounds were internal or if the creature had done more damage than he could comprehend.

Tears welled in his eyes, but he forced them back. He had to stay strong for her. Lifting the girl into his arms, he cradled her fragile body against him.

As they moved, the younger girl, who had led Filadelfo to the scene, anxiously tugged at his robe. 'What do I do, Father?'

'Run ahead,' he urged, his voice trembling slightly. 'Find Mother Valentina, tell her to prepare the infirmary—quickly!'

As the girl sprinted away, he whispered under his breath, 'You're safe now. I've got you.'

Before leaving the glasshouse, the girl in his arms stirred slightly, her voice no more than a whisper. 'Numquam obliviscaris. Numquam interrogare prohibere. Ille in te computatis.'

Father Filadelfo strained to hear her Latin words. 'You must never forget. Never stop questioning. He's counting on you,' she murmured before slipping into unconsciousness.

'I promise,' he said softly, though he wasn't sure what exactly he was promising.

Father Filadelfo was a young priest, only ordained the year before. He wasn't a particularly strong man, as evidenced by his struggle to keep holding onto the girl so as not to drop her. He had to stop many times on the way to get a better grip. As the girl went in and out of consciousness, she kept asking, 'Was it just a dream?'

'No, child,' said the priest. 'No, it wasn't a dream.'

'Mother Valentina? Where's Mother Valentina?' asked the girl as she reached the nurses' station.

'What is it, little angel?' asked one nurse.

'She's hurt. Father Filadelfo is carrying her to you. He told me to run ahead to tell you—she's bleeding. So much blood.'

Amazed and taken aback by what they had just heard, they all sprang up from their stations and grabbed a bed to rush out to meet them.

'Go get Mother Superior,' ordered one nurse to another.

As Father Filadelfo reached the infirmary wing, the nurses had already started to wheel out a bed to meet him. He gently placed the girl down on the bed, and the monastery's doctor immediately took over.

'What happened, Father Filadelfo?' asked the doctor.

With a shaky voice, he muttered, 'She was violated, violently.'

'Who did this?' asked Mother Superior as she joined the convoy back to the ward.

'It was... the Monsignor,' sighed the priest.

Everyone gasped aloud.

'But it was like he was possessed. It wasn't him,' blubbered Filadelfo.

'Well, was it the Monsignor or not, Father Filadelfo?' asked Mother Superior.

'It was him, but when I arrived, it was what looked like an angel wearing his cloth.'

'Where is he? I'll kill him myself!' screamed Mother Superior as she started to storm off.

'He's... dead,' said Filadelfo. 'I... I... I killed him. It was an accident, I swear on my life it was an accident. I was trying to stop this creature from abusing the child any more than it did.'

'Dead?' exclaimed Mother Superior.

'Yes, dead,' said Filadelfo.

'Come with me, Father. Tell me what happened,' said Sister Serafina.

As they began walking out of the infirmary towards a prayer chapel nearby, she instructed another sister to take care of the other child.

'Clean her up and make sure she is all right. Check her over, put a blanket around her to prevent chilling, and don't let her eat or drink anything. And for the love of our Lord, make sure she doesn't go to sleep; she may be in shock too.'

Once they were alone in the chapel, Sister Serafina asked Father Filadelfo to take a seat and walk her through what had happened.

'I was praying upstairs in the oratory when little Elena interrupted my devotions, telling me that someone was being hurt in the garden. I ran after the child, not sure what to expect. When we made it to the glasshouse...' Father Filadelfo faded off.

'What happened at the glasshouse?' asked Sister Serafina.

'When I got there,' said Filadelfo, 'I saw a creature that was all white, glowing like the sun but wearing the Monsignor's robes. When it looked right at me, it was like it was relishing getting caught. And then it looked at me like I was next. Without thinking, I jumped on its back to pull it off, but I didn't realise that when I landed on it, my crucifix pierced its spine and killed it. Then all the light disappeared, and it was just the Monsignor on top of the girl. But I swear it wasn't him committing this crime. He was possessed by something—something that, if I saw it in the garden on any other occasion, I would have thought it was an angel of God and laid prostrate before it.'

Bewildered, Sister Serafina could only manage, 'Ok, Father. It's all ok now. Would you like tea to help calm your nerves?'

Tea was a euphemism for whisky in most monasteries throughout Italy.

'I might need the whole pot,' said Father Filadelfo.

It hadn't taken long for the police and paramedics to arrive at the monastery after being informed of the day's events. Police took statements, and the young girl was transported to a nearby hospital that could handle such sensitive and psychological trauma victims. The Police Inspector questioned Father Filadelfo personally as a favour to the Church, so as not to exacerbate the scandal with gossip.

A phone call came into the Mother Superior's chambers from the Archbishop's office, advising that Archbishop Bussi would like to come to the monastery to investigate the allegations against the Monsignor and talk to the priest who had witnessed the events.

After the inspector finished taking statements and the paramedics took the young girl to the hospital, Father Filadelfo walked back to the kitchen and sat at the table, staring off into the distance, still struggling to process what he'd witnessed.

Father Filadelfo was interrupted by Sister Chiara. 'I just received a phone call from the Archbishop's office, advising that Archbishop Bussi himself is on his way to the abbey to speak with you.'

'Do you think His Excellency would believe your story?' asked Mother Valentina, as she also walked into the kitchen.

'I have nothing to hide,' said Filadelfo. 'I saw what I saw, and I won't allow anyone to gaslight me into thinking otherwise.'

'I think I'll go and take a nap,' said the priest.

'I just can't—'

'Ok, good idea,' said Mother Valentina, interrupting him. 'And while you're there, pray to the Almighty for strength. I think you're going to need it.'

Taking the short walk back via the garden to his chambers, he couldn't get the image out of his head—that what looked like an angel of God was, in fact, the perpetrator of such a grievous crime. How could this be? Were more angels falling from grace? Did this happen often? I thought it only happened in ancient times, he mused.

Getting confused by his own questions, Father Filadelfo lay on his bed, still contemplating all that he'd just witnessed as he started to drift off to sleep.

'WHERE IS HE?' demanded a powerful voice emanating from the entrance. 'WHERE IS THE MONSIGNOR?' the voice demanded again.

Hearing the shouts, the sisters ran out of their respective stations to see the commotion. When they reached the source of the demands, they were confronted by what looked like a small army. Front and centre was the Archbishop, flanked by at least twenty guards.

'Where is the Monsignor?' demanded the Archbishop again as he walked down the corridor, growing rather impatient now that he'd had to ask three times.

'I... I... I'll take you to him—his body, Your Excellency,' perked up a young sister. 'I'll take you to his body.'

'Thank you, my dear, thank you.'

Walking hastily through the chapel doors, the Archbishop exclaimed, 'YOU HAVE HIM IN HERE? THIS IS A HOLY PLACE OF GOD; IT SHOULD NOT BE DEFILED BY THIS CREATURE'S PRESENCE. REMOVE HIM AT ONCE!'

'Where shall we place his body then, Your Excellency?'

'I DON'T CARE! ON THE KITCHEN TABLE, IF AVAILABLE, BUT...' He paused, remembering his need to compose himself. Taking a deep, calming breath, he uttered in a more civilised tone, 'Anywhere but here.'

"Yes, Your Excellency."

The Captain of the guards barked, "GUARDS! Assist in moving this man to a more suitable place. Quickly, brothers, let's put him in his vestry," said the Lieutenant.

"I can't believe they thought to put him in the chapel," muttered the Archbishop to no one in particular.

Confused by this outburst, but in blind obedience, the remaining guards agreed by all stomping their right foot once.

Six of the guards had gone up to the body lying on the small trolley used to hold coffins at funerals, known as a wheel bier. Five of them only saw a man lying there; however, the sixth saw something else. He saw the angel that Father Filadelfo had seen raping the young girl in the glasshouse—glowing with light, alive—and looking right at him with what appeared to be a command. Discomforted by this, he drew his sword, spinning around to gain more momentum and enough time to say, "Vade Retro Satanas!"—which means "Get thee behind me, Satan!"—and, with his sword now raised high, he bought down the sword slamming it down on the neck of the Archbishop, severing his head clean from his body.

In a flash, the guard realised it was just a thought, a daydream from the dark recesses of his psyche where no one was allowed to venture while holding such an important station within the Church. He hadn't actually killed the Archbishop after all. It seemed so real, he thought to himself, as he helped lift the Monsignor's body from the wheel bier with the others. That's crazy... it seemed so real. Am I losing my mind? he asked himself.

As the guards began walking out of the chapel in a solemn manner, they all noticed a sweet smell infusing the air. They looked at each other for validation, confirming they could all smell it.

"Maybe the cook has something nice for us," perked one guard. "Maybe," they all conceded.

Continuing down the corridor to the Monsignor's room, they passed the Chief Inspector, who stopped the procession and asked what they were doing.

"You can't just move the body!" exclaimed the Inspector.

"Well," said the Archbishop, "we can't leave the body in the chapel. It's sacrilegious to honour such a beast that way. We're taking him back to his vestry."

"But you've already broken protocol by moving him once already—from the glasshouse to the chapel. Now you're moving him again to his room? Where next? Perhaps the library? This is madness! I came to help ensure the Church is protected from idle gossip and speculation, and you're moving the body again! How can I do my job when you're constantly getting in the way?"

"You're right," said the Archbishop. "We promise we'll get out of your way so you can conduct your investigation. The Church appreciates your consideration and respect."

"Thank you," said the Inspector. "The Coroner will be here shortly to collect his body anyway."

"Guards!" the Captain barked. "Assist the Inspector in anything he needs and ensure no one, except the Inspector and the Coroner, gains access to his room. You two," he said with a nod, "stay here and guard the door. No one is to enter. Understood?"

The two guards stood at attention, simultaneously grunting and stamping their right foot in acknowledgement of their compliance before taking their places on either side of the Monsignor's vestry door.

"Mother Superior"

"Yes, Your Excellency!"

"You're in charge of the monastery until a suitable replacement can be found for the Monsignor."

"Of course, Your Excellency."

"Now, where is the priest who kill… um… found the Monsignor?" The Archbishop paused, careful not to implicate the priest in front of the Chief Inspector.

"He's in his vestry, resting," responded one sister.

"OK, let him be for now, but I would like to speak with him as soon as he is available."

"Yes, of course," said the Mother Superior.

"Captain!"

"Yes, Your Excellency?"

"Place two guards at his door, and as soon as he awakens, escort him to me."

"Yes, Your Excellency." With a nod, the Captain commanded, "You and you, stand guard as His Excellency has requested."

"Are you needing anything else, Inspector?" asked the Archbishop. "No, I'm OK for now," the Inspector replied.

"Good. Mother Superior, would you please organise lunch and make sure the men are well looked after?"

"Certainly, Your Excellency."

"Will you and the... men," she said with trepidation at the sheer number of strong men surrounding the sisters, "be staying long?"

"A few days, maybe. Hopefully, we can resolve this unfortunate matter in due time so we all can get back to our respective duties."

The Mother Superior bowed her head in submission. "I'll personally see that you and the men are well accommodated."

"Thank you, Mother Superior," said the Archbishop. He repeated his thanks again as he faded into thought, gazing out the window while the gravity of what had happened began to sink in.

"Sister Serafina?"

"Yes, Mother," she replied.

"See that the men have suitable accommodation, and tell the cook we have guests for a few days."

"Yes, Mother," Serafina said, bowing her head slightly before turning and heading towards the kitchen.

"Sisters, come, follow me," ordered the Mother Superior as she started walking towards their private quarters. Upon reaching the quarters, she turned to Sister Lucia.

"Can you gather all the other sisters and bring them here immediately? Those who are caring for others I will see later."

"Yes, Mother." Sister Lucia turned and scurried off to gather the others.

As the sisters began filing into their quarters, Mother Superior addressed them with a grave tone. "Never be alone while the guards are here. Of course, they have taken a vow of celibacy, but they are still mortal men, and men will be men."

Some of the nuns began to giggle at the thought.

"So, for the time they are here, no one is to be alone. Always stay in groups of two or more, and if one of these men propositions you — or worse — you are to come straight to me and tell me everything. I'll deal with the devil myself. Understood?"

"Yes, Mother," they all replied in unison, though some sounded clearly disappointed.

"You, too, made vows. It will serve you well to remember that, Sisters. You are brides of Christ and no one else's."

"Yes, Mother," they replied, singularly this time.

Father Filadelfo's sleep was restless, plagued with vivid nightmares of the glowing figure, the screams, and the horrifying silence that followed. As he thrashed in his bed, flashes of the glasshouse, the blinding light, and the grotesque transformation of the Monsignor blurred in his mind. Suddenly, his eyes shot open, heart pounding, drenched in sweat. Dusk had already settled, casting long shadows across his small room. He rubbed his temples, trying to shake off the weight of the day.

A sharp knock at the door startled him, pulling him back to reality.

"Father Filadelfo?" came Sister Chiara's voice from the hallway. "His Excellency, Archbishop Bussi, is awaiting you in the kitchen. He's... requested your presence."

Still groggy, Filadelfo sat up, blinking into the dim light. The events of the day hung heavy in the air, and he could already feel the gnawing dread creeping back into his chest. He hadn't even processed what he had witnessed, and now he was being summoned by the Archbishop himself. The thought sent a shiver through him.

He quickly dressed, his hands trembling slightly as he fastened his collar. The weight of his crucifix felt heavier than usual, almost suffocating. He glanced at the clock—7:30 p.m. How had so much time passed since the incident?

Opening the door, he found Sister Chiara waiting for him, her expression a mixture of concern and urgency.

"I'll take you to him," she said softly, casting a brief, anxious glance at the floor before turning to lead the way.

The hallways of the monastery were bathed in the golden light of dusk, and the usual peaceful silence seemed to carry an ominous weight. As they descended the narrow stone staircase, Filadelfo's mind raced. How could he even begin to explain what had happened? And what was the Archbishop going to do about it?

They reached the kitchen, the soft hum of conversation growing louder as they approached. Archbishop Bussi sat at the head of the long wooden table, a steaming cup of tea in front of him. He was a tall, imposing man with piercing eyes that seemed to see right through Filadelfo. His presence alone commanded the room.

"Father Filadelfo," the Archbishop greeted, gesturing for him to sit. His voice was calm, but his sharp gaze didn't leave Filadelfo for a second. "We have much to discuss."

Filadelfo sat down slowly, his body stiff with tension. The Archbishop leaned forward slightly, his fingers steepled, watching Filadelfo with a calculating intensity.

"Your Excellency..." Filadelfo began, his voice cracking slightly from exhaustion and nerves. "I don't even know how to start."

The Archbishop's expression remained impassive, though his eyes seemed to darken with something unreadable. "Take your time, Father. Start from the beginning. I need to hear every detail."

Filadelfo's throat felt dry as he began to recount the events in halting breaths. He told the Archbishop about little Elena's frantic plea, the strange, overpowering light in the glasshouse, and the horrific scene that unfolded before him—the Monsignor, possessed by something far beyond human understanding. As he spoke, his words tumbled out faster, desperation leaking into his voice as he tried to make sense of what he had witnessed.

When he reached the part about the crucifix melting into the creature's spine, the Archbishop's brow furrowed slightly. His hands tightened around the handle of his cup, but he said nothing, allowing Filadelfo to continue.

"I don't know what it was... or if it was even real," Filadelfo said, his voice shaking. "It was like he was possessed by something ancient, something... evil."

Archbishop Bussi leaned back in his chair, folding his hands in his lap. His expression remained calm, though his eyes betrayed a glimmer of something—recognition, perhaps. "Father," he began, his voice measured, "this isn't the first time the Church has dealt with... strange occurrences. But this—" He paused, choosing his words carefully. "What you're describing aligns with certain... records. But even for us, this is unprecedented."

Father Filadelfo felt a cold shiver crawl down his spine. He'd expected doubt, scepticism, but there was none of that in the Archbishop's voice. Instead, there was an unsettling understanding.

Just as the Archbishop was about to continue, the kitchen door creaked open. Mother Valentina stepped in, her face pale, holding a phone in her hand.

"Your Excellency..." she began hesitantly, glancing between the two men. "I just received a call. From Rome." The Archbishop's eyes narrowed, sensing something was amiss. "Rome?" he asked, his voice calm but laced with curiosity.

Mother Valentina nodded, swallowing hard. "The Vatican. They've asked for Father Filadelfo... immediately."

The room fell into a heavy silence. The words hung in the air like a curse. Father Filadelfo felt his stomach drop as if the floor had vanished beneath him. The Archbishop, blindsided, sat straighter in his chair, his face betraying a moment of disbelief before he composed himself.

"The Vatican?" Filadelfo stammered, his voice barely above a whisper. "They want to see... me?"

The Archbishop's jaw clenched, his eyes flickering with something between frustration and unease. He hadn't expected this, not so soon, not in the middle of their conversation. "It seems they've taken an immediate interest in your... experience," he said, his voice measured. "This wasn't something I anticipated."

For a brief moment, the Archbishop's usually composed expression faltered, replaced by a hint of something Filadelfo couldn't quite read—was it fear? Or resignation?

He turned to Mother Valentina, his voice lowering. "What exactly did they say?"

"They're sending transport, and he's to attend immediately. That was all, Your Excellency."

For what seemed like hours, Father Filadelfo sat at the kitchen table, staring blankly at the untouched cup of tea in front of him. The events of the last few hours haunted him. The creature—the Monsignor—its body lay motionless, but its impact lingered. He couldn't shake the image of the glowing figure, the blinding light, and the horrifying moment when he realized the man was possessed by something otherworldly.

The weight of what had happened, of what he'd done, hung heavy on his shoulders. Could he really face the Vatican? Could he explain the unexplainable to those who held the highest authority in the Church? He ran a trembling hand through his hair.

"The Pope himself has summoned me." These words felt like a hammer blow. The Vatican's involvement meant this was far bigger than anything he could have imagined.

Before Father Filadelfo could process everything, the sound of an approaching vehicle rumbled outside. One of the Archbishop's guards glanced through the window to see a sleek, black SUV pulling up to the monastery's front entrance. Under the dim streetlight, its tinted windows gave it a secretive, almost menacing aura.

"They're here," whispered Mother Valentina, her usually composed face marred by tension. "You need to go now. They won't wait."

Filadelfo felt his heart hammering in his chest, but he nodded. There was no time to waste. Grabbing his coat, he stepped out of the small kitchen and into the cold night air. His phone buzzed—a text notification. He glanced down at the screen.

Subject: URGENT: Confidential Briefing
From: Vatican Secretary
To: Father Filadelfo
You will be briefed en route. Under no circumstances discuss what you witnessed until you reach the Vatican. Orders direct from His Holiness.

He slipped the phone back into his pocket, his hand trembling slightly as he did. A Vatican guard, dressed not in ceremonial robes but in modern tactical gear, stood by the SUV.

"Father Filadelfo?" the guard asked, his voice professional but cold. Filadelfo nodded. "Please, come with us," the guard said, opening the rear door of the vehicle. "I'll need your phone."

Compliantly, he surrendered his phone and got in. The interior was dark and cool, with the soft hum of technology in the background. Another guard sat inside, typing something on a tablet, barely acknowledging the priest's entrance.

As soon as Filadelfo stepped inside, the door shut with a muted thud, sealing him off from the outside world. The car pulled away from the monastery, the sound of gravel crunching beneath the tyres fading into the distance.

They drove in silence for a while, the lights of the town blurring past the windows. Filadelfo stared out, lost in thought, trying to comprehend how his quiet, uneventful life had spiralled into something so incomprehensible.

Suddenly, the guard beside him handed over a tablet. "This is for you, Father. The Pope has sent a personal message. It's encrypted— you'll need to scan your Vatican ID for access."

With shaking hands, Filadelfo retrieved his ID card from his wallet and scanned it. The screen flashed to life, revealing a brief but chilling message from the Pope himself:

Father Filadelfo, I trust you will understand the gravity of the situation. The Vatican has dealt with... disturbances like this before, but rarely one so severe. There are forces at work far beyond our reach. You have witnessed what few have lived to speak of. The world may depend on what happens next.

As the car approached the highway leading toward the Vatican, the vehicle's internal security system locked all the doors. Filadelfo's heart raced. He couldn't escape even if he wanted to.

Just as he closed the message, the car slowed abruptly. Up ahead, a set of headlights pierced the darkness. Two black SUVs were parked across the road, their engines still running. A man dressed in an impeccably tailored suit stepped into the light, flanked by several others. Their faces were obscured, but their presence was unmistakably deliberate.

"Who are they?" Filadelfo whispered, more to himself than to anyone else.

The guard beside him tightened his grip on his gun. "No one we were expecting."

The SUV rolled to a stop, and for a moment, time seemed to stretch endlessly. The men outside were waiting for something—or someone. The tension was palpable, the air thick with anticipation.

Without warning, the driver turned to Filadelfo. "Father, stay inside. No matter what happens."

The door locks clicked again, this time with a resounding finality. Filadelfo's mind raced, his pulse pounding in his ears. Who were these men? Why had they intercepted them?

Suddenly, the figure in the suit stepped forward, his voice muffled but sharp as it cut through the night. "Father Filadelfo, step out of the vehicle. We've been expecting you."

His words sent a chill down Filadelfo's spine. Expecting him? But how? Before he could react, the SUV's engine roared to life again, the driver ignoring the command.

"We have orders to get you to the Vatican—no matter what."

The car lurched forward, speeding past the barricade of black SUVs. Filadelfo's heart thundered in his chest as they tore down the empty road, the men in suits disappearing into the night behind them, making no effort to chase.

But something about the figure's parting words echoed in his mind. We've been expecting you.

As the Vatican's towering spires came into view on the horizon, dread settled deep within him. Whatever waited for him inside those ancient walls was more than just a mystery.

It was a reckoning.

Chapter 16

Dark Forces

The black SUV roared through the cobbled streets of Rome, the Vatican's spires piercing the night sky like silent sentinels. Father Filadelfo sat stiffly in the backseat, his hands clenched tightly in his lap. Filadelfo felt the edges of his mind unravelling. He gripped the seatbelt as though it were a rosary, his lips moving silently in prayer though the words faltered on his tongue. What had I seen? The question gnawed at him, but no answer came. The Monsignor's face—twisted in pain, or perhaps ecstasy—flashed before him, followed by the blazing light that seemed to sear into his very soul. Was it truly divine, or something darker cloaked in glory? A fresh wave of nausea gripped him, his faith teetering under the weight of confusion. The silence in the car was suffocating, and even the driver's calm presence felt like a veil, hiding truths Filadelfo was not ready to confront. Every instinct told him that nothing good awaited him at the end of this journey.

The Vatican's gates loomed ahead, wrought iron and imposing, their intricate designs seeming to shimmer in the moonlight. As the SUV slowed, the guards on duty waved them through without so much as a glance. The driver's silence was unnerving, and Filadelfo felt the weight of unseen eyes as the vehicle rolled deeper into the Vatican grounds.

Finally, the car came to a halt in a secluded courtyard. The engine cut off, and the driver stepped out. Moving swiftly to Filadelfo's side, he opened the door and motioned for him to step out. "This way, Father," the driver said curtly, his voice betraying neither warmth nor malice.

Filadelfo hesitated for only a moment before stepping into the chill of the night. His shoes crunched softly against the gravel as he followed the driver up a set of wide stone steps. At the top stood two Vatican guards, their faces set like stone, their eyes giving nothing away.

The driver exchanged a brief nod with the guards before turning back to Filadelfo. "They'll take you from here." Without another word, he descended the steps, disappearing into the shadows.

One of the guards stepped forward. "Father Filadelfo," he said, his voice low and formal. "Follow us."

The massive doors behind them groaned open, revealing a long corridor lit by flickering torches. The air inside was heavy with incense, and the walls were lined with ancient tapestries depicting battles between angels and demons. Filadelfo's footsteps echoed faintly as he walked between the two guards, his unease growing with every step. He wanted to ask where they were taking him, but something about their silence warned him against speaking.

After what felt like an eternity, they arrived at another set of doors, smaller but no less ornate. One of the guards knocked twice, the sound reverberating in the stillness. A moment later, the doors opened, and Filadelfo was ushered inside.

The chamber was dimly lit, the soft glow of candles casting dancing shadows across the high, vaulted ceiling. At the far end of the room stood a desk, its surface cluttered with manuscripts and relics. Behind it sat a figure shrouded in shadow, the faint outline of his silhouette barely visible in the candlelight.

"Father Filadelfo," the figure spoke, his voice calm yet carrying an undeniable authority. "You have seen much."

Filadelfo's breath caught in his throat. "Your Holiness?" he ventured, though he could not see the man's face clearly.

The figure leaned forward slightly, but the shadows seemed to deepen, obscuring his features further. "You are not here to ask questions, my son. You are here to listen. What you witnessed was no accident. There are forces at work—forces older than the Church itself, forces that have long sought to unseat the divine order."

The words hung heavy in the air, and Filadelfo felt a cold sweat break out on his brow. "I... I don't understand," he stammered.

"You do not need to," the voice replied, a hint of finality in its tone. "Your role in this has only just begun. You will be guided from here, but know this—silence is your salvation. Speak of what you have seen to no one, not even in prayer."

Before Filadelfo could respond, the figure gestured to one of the guards. "Take him to the dormitory. He will remain under observation."

The guard stepped forward, his hand lightly resting on Filadelfo's shoulder. "Come, Father."

As the guard led Filadelfo out of the chamber, the shadowed figure turned back to his desk. His hand rested on a small medallion engraved with an unfamiliar symbol—two crossed keys intertwined with a serpent. The flickering candlelight played tricks on the design, making it seem as though the serpent writhed beneath his fingers.

At the same moment, hundreds of miles away in the Monsignor's office, Archbishop Bussi stared at a faded parchment bearing the same symbol. He traced the lines absently, his thoughts a storm of questions. The weight of what he had discovered over decades pressed against his chest like a vice. Somewhere deep inside, he knew the truth was already spiralling out of his control.

Bussi had been collecting information on the Order of the Hidden Cross for decades, though he would never dare admit it aloud. Even within the confines of the Vatican's most secretive chambers, there were eyes. Ears. He had learned this the hard way, as a young priest just beginning to understand the darker undercurrents within the Church's walls. The Order, he had discovered through whispers and half-burned letters, had been guarding something—no, some-one—for centuries. A man. A man who, if freed, could unravel the very fabric of the Church's foundations.

For years, Bussi had been careful and methodical in his search for answers. He had built a lifetime's worth of trust, rising quiet-ly through the ranks, always staying in the Church's good graces while secretly gathering scraps of knowledge that few dared even acknowledge.

But it had all started with a dream. A dream that had haunted him since his early days in the priesthood. He had seen a boy—no older than ten—holding a key in his hand, standing before a massive door etched with ancient symbols. Behind the door lay the truth, a truth so dangerous that its mere existence threatened to bring ev-erything crashing down. Bussi had spent his life searching for that boy, never realising until recently that the child existed not in this world but in another—a parallel universe.

It was Beris—an unearthly creature sent by Joshua Carpenter—who had revealed this to him. Beris had appeared to Bussi during his meditations, a messenger from a dimension far beyond his un-derstanding. Joshua, a boy whose own fate was intertwined with the very fabric of the universe, had tasked Bussi with a mission:

find the man imprisoned beneath the Vatican and set him free. But the task was dangerous. Even knowing the truth about the Order of the Hidden Cross could bring death.

That's why Bussi had been cautious. He couldn't act rashly. He couldn't ask questions openly. But he had kept his eyes and ears open, and now, after years of quiet investigation, he was closer to the truth than ever before.

Earlier that night, Beris had appeared to Bussi again, as he often did during times of meditation. The small being's presence had become a comfort to the Archbishop despite the otherworldly nature of their connection.

"Joshua has one last message," Beris had said, his voice soft but clear. "You must ensure that Filadelfo is placed in the Order of the Hidden Cross."

Bussi had blinked, confused. "The Order? But... no outsider has ever been allowed in. They are raised from birth, isolated, indoctrinated."

"Joshua speaks the truth," Beris had insisted, his eyes glimmering with an almost impossible depth. "Filadelfo is essential to the plan. The man they guard—Yehoshua—cannot be freed without him."

Bussi had always been a man of action despite his many years in the Church. His instincts told him something was wrong the moment Father Filadelfo left under the Vatican guards' escort. Bussi had done his best to convince the Pope that Filadelfo needed guidance, protection even, but as soon as the guards had whisked him away, something deep inside gnawed at him. There was a darkness swirling around this entire affair.

Decades of whispered rumours, unspoken truths, and cryptic encounters with the mysterious Order of the Hidden Cross had led him to this point, and now Filadelfo—an innocent, confused priest—was being dragged into the heart of that storm.

Bussi wasted no time. Without thinking, he threw on his coat, hurried down the steps of his private office, and raced to the garage. His hands shook as he started the engine of his car, the cold night air already misting his breath. He knew where they were taking Filadelfo. To the Vatican. To the heart of everything.

The streets were empty, eerily quiet, as he tore through the winding roads. His mind buzzed with a thousand thoughts, but all of them came back to the same terrifying conclusion: he couldn't let this happen. Filadelfo had seen too much, and Bussi knew all too well what happened to those who saw too much. He couldn't let the Vatican swallow him whole.

After driving for what felt like an eternity, Bussi spotted the guards' SUV up ahead. His heart pounded. He was getting close. But just as he neared the vehicle, something strange caught his attention. Up ahead, two black SUVs were parked across the road, engines still running, their headlights casting long shadows in the night. A man in a tailored suit stepped out of one of the vehicles, flanked by several others who remained in the shadows.

Bussi's stomach twisted with unease. He brought his car to a slow stop, his headlights casting just enough light to see the men clearly. One of them turned, his face a mask of cold detachment, and met Bussi's gaze. It was as if they were waiting for him, just as they had been waiting for Filadelfo.

The moment stretched out, the cold air thick with tension. Bussi didn't move. Neither did the men. Then, with a faint nod from the suited man, they seemed to acknowledge each other.

No words were exchanged. It wasn't necessary. Whatever they had come for, they weren't going to interfere with Bussi. He wasn't the one they were after. He understood that much. And yet, there was something deeper in their silent acknowledgement—something dark, foreboding.

Without a second glance, Bussi slammed on the gas, speeding off towards the Vatican, his pulse racing. As he glanced in the rear-view mirror, the two SUVs and the men standing in the road seemed to dissipate into the cold night air, vanishing like phantoms. It was as if they had never been there at all.

The moment Bussi arrived at the Vatican, he rushed through the grand hallways, his robes billowing behind him as he made his way to the Pope's private chambers. He had been summoned to see His Holiness, but he already knew this conversation would be unlike any other they had shared. The Pope was a wise man, but even he couldn't see the full picture—not like Bussi could.

After being granted an audience, Bussi was escorted into the room where the Pope sat in his high-backed chair, his gaze distant, yet piercing, as Archbishop Bussi approached. The candlelight flick-ered in the dim room, casting tall, wavering shadows along the walls. The scent of incense was heavy, almost suffocating, as if the air itself held ancient secrets that should remain buried.

"Your Holiness," Bussi bowed deeply, his voice hushed but urgent. "I come with a matter of great importance. It is about Father Fil-adelfo."

The Pope remained silent for a moment, his hands folded togeth-er in his lap. His eyes, though clouded with age, glimmered with something beneath their surface—something knowing. He exhaled slowly as if preparing himself to speak of things long hidden.

"Yes," he said finally, his voice softer than Bussi expected—a voice weighed down by centuries of knowledge. "I have heard. Filadelfo witnessed… something."

The pause was deliberate, and for a brief second, Bussi thought he saw the flames of the candles flicker unnaturally, casting shadows that twisted on the walls. The Pope's gaze shifted, almost imper-ceptibly, to a dark corner of the room where no light could reach.

Bussi swallowed.

"It was more than just 'something', Your Holiness. He saw things no man should ever see—things that the Church has spent centuries hiding."

The Pope's eyes darkened, but not with surprise. Instead, there was a resignation in them, as though he had been expecting this moment. The faintest smile tugged at the corner of his lips, but it was not a smile of warmth.

"You speak dangerous words, Archbishop," the Pope said, his tone soft but carrying an undeniable weight. "Even for one such as yourself."

The Pope's voice softened almost imperceptibly. "There is much the Church guards, Archbishop. Some secrets even I do not dare to name aloud." His gaze drifted toward a small iron box on a nearby table, its lock sealed with intricate carvings. The box was unassuming to an untrained eye, but Bussi's breath hitched. He had seen it only once before, years ago, in the hidden archives of the Vatican. It was said to contain the original decree establishing the Order of the Hidden Cross—an order shrouded in whispers and half-truths.

The Pope returned his gaze to Bussi, his expression unreadable. "You believe yourself prepared to walk this path. Be certain, Archbishop, that it is not the path that will consume you but the shadows it hides."

"I know what will happen to Filadelfo if we do nothing. He will vanish, like the others before him. The Church will erase him. I have seen this pattern before, Your Holiness."

The Pope leaned forward, his eyes locking onto Bussi's with an intensity that made the Archbishop's skin crawl.

"And you believe you understand the forces at play here? You think the Church has not weighed the cost of keeping these... truths hidden?"

Bussi's throat tightened. There was something in the Pope's voice—a knowledge deeper than the Vatican archives, something ancient and dark.

The Pope's next words were like a whisper from another world.

"There are things, Archbishop—powers older than Christianity, older than Rome. Forces beyond us. Beyond Filadelfo. Beyond me." The Pope's voice dropped, his next words barely audible. "The Order does not guard these truths lightly."

His voice dropped, becoming almost inaudible.

"Not even by me."

Bussi felt a chill slide down his spine, the cold creeping into his bones. For a moment, the shadows around the room seemed to deepen as though the walls themselves were listening, waiting.

"Your Holiness," Bussi's voice was trembling, but he steadied himself. "I know the dangers. I have spent decades gathering what little I could. I have seen enough to understand the risk. But I believe there is another way. Filadelfo's disappearance would only raise questions—dangerous questions. The press, the people—they will seek answers. But if we were to cleanse him… erase his memory… we could control the narrative."

The Pope's lips pressed together in a thin line, his gaze turning towards the flickering candle beside him. Its flame danced unnaturally, casting strange, fleeting symbols in the shadows.

"Erase his memory?" the Pope echoed, his voice colder now, almost detached. "You speak of the ritual."

Bussi nodded. "Yes, Your Holiness. The ritual has not been used in decades, but it is the only way. We cannot make him vanish without consequence. But if we cleanse his mind, if we rewrite his reality, we can place him somewhere safe. Where he will no longer be a threat."

The Pope's silence was thick, palpable. He rose slowly from his seat, his robe brushing against the floor, and moved to the window. Outside, the Vatican was bathed in darkness, the ancient walls seeming to close in around them both.

"There is a reason," the Pope began, "why the ritual has not been used in so long." His voice grew softer, but the weight of it pressed down on Bussi's chest. "It is not just dangerous, Archbishop. It is cruel. It does not simply erase memories. It unravels the soul."

Bussi felt a knot tighten in his stomach. He had heard rumours of what the ritual could do, of priests who had gone mad, of minds shattered beyond repair. But he had also heard of its success. He clung to the latter, desperate.

"The alternative is worse," Bussi pressed, stepping closer. "To vanish him without a trace is to sentence him to death. This way, we can still save him. Even if the process is… harsh."

The Pope turned his head slightly, his eyes narrowing.

"Do you truly believe that you are saving him? Or are you simply afraid of what he might reveal?"

Bussi swallowed hard. "I am trying to prevent the collapse of everything we've worked for, Your Holiness. If word of what Filadelfo saw spreads, the consequences will be catastrophic. We cannot let the world know what lies beneath our feet. I beg of you, let me perform the ritual."

The Pope stared at Bussi for a long, unnerving moment, his face unreadable. Then, finally, he spoke, his voice almost a whisper.

"You have seen much, Archbishop. Far more than I suspect you were ever meant to see."

Bussi's heart skipped a beat. There was something in the Pope's tone—an acknowledgement that perhaps Bussi had stumbled onto something far beyond his comprehension. Something that should have remained hidden.

"You tread dangerous ground," the Pope continued, his eyes flickering with an emotion Bussi couldn't quite place. "But perhaps you are right. Perhaps this is the lesser of two evils. But understand this, Archbishop..." His voice dropped to a chilling whisper. "There are forces at work here, forces you cannot hope to control. The ritual may cleanse his memory, but it will not cleanse the truth. That truth will always remain. It lingers. In the shadows. In the dark corners of this very room."

For a moment, the Pope's eyes seemed to gleam, almost as if reflecting the flickering candlelight. But Bussi could swear that the darkness in the room shifted, a shadow curling at the edges of his vision.

"I will grant you permission to perform the ritual," the Pope said, his voice returning to its usual calm. "But be warned, Archbishop. You may find that in your pursuit of saving him, you lose something far greater."

Bussi felt the weight of the words settle over him like a shroud. He bowed deeply, hiding the tremor in his voice.

"Thank you, Your Holiness. I will proceed with caution."

As he turned to leave, the Pope's voice stopped him one last time.

"And Archbishop," the Pope said softly, "pray that what you have set in motion does not consume you as well."

Bussi turned back briefly to see the Pope still standing by the window, his silhouette framed against the darkened sky. For a fleeting moment, Bussi thought he saw the faintest trace of a smile on the Pope's lips, but it was gone as quickly as it had appeared.

With that, Bussi left the room, his mind buzzing with the weight of what had just transpired. The permission was granted, but something far more ominous now clung to him—something ancient and unspoken, lurking just beneath the surface.

Bussi bowed deeply.

"Thank you, Your Holiness. I won't fail."

The following morning, Filadelfo stood at the entrance to the ancient monastery, a letter from the Pope himself clutched in his hand. The vast, imposing structure loomed before him, its towering stone walls bathed in the pale light of dawn. The air was cold, sharp, and carried a sense of finality that settled deep in Filadelfo's bones.

He had been summoned to see His Holiness, and now, after the ritual, he had been placed in the Order of the Hidden Cross. The details of the last few days were hazy in his mind. He remembered standing before the Pope, feeling the weight of judgment on him. And then, there had been… something. A ritual, a cleansing. He couldn't recall exactly what had happened.

Filadelfo touched his forehead absentmindedly, his fingers brushing against skin that felt oddly sensitive, as though it had been burned. Fragments of the ritual flickered in his mind—voices chanting in an ancient language, hands pressing on his temples, and blinding light so bright it seemed to cut into his soul. There had been a moment, brief but visceral when he had felt something leave him—something ripped away, leaving behind a hollowness he couldn't explain.

The details eluded him. The harder he tried to recall, the more they slipped through his grasp like sand spilling between his fingers. All he knew was the ache deep in his chest, and the nagging sensation that whatever was gone had been vital to who he was. The Pope's warning rang faintly in his mind, though he could no longer remember the exact words. Only their weight remained.

But he knew one thing: he had been assigned a new role. A role that would see him live out the rest of his days beneath the Vatican, away from the world, away from everything he had known.

As he stepped through the grand entrance of the monastery, the heavy doors closed behind him with a soft thud, sealing his fate. Inside, the cold stone corridors stretched out before him, silent, endless.

The air inside the monastery clung to Filadelfo like a damp cloth, heavy with the scent of cold stone and something faintly metallic. The sound of his footsteps echoed down the long, arched corridor, but the space swallowed the noise, making it feel distant, as though the building itself were alive and listening.

He clutched the Pope's letter tightly, its edges curling from his grip. His eyes darted to the towering walls, where faint carvings seemed to emerge and retreat into the shadows with each flicker of torchlight. Shapes that looked like angels, yet twisted, their wings too sharp, their eyes too hollow. "Follow," a voice commanded, cutting through his trance.

He looked up to see a robed figure waiting, face hidden beneath a hood. Without another word, the figure turned and began walking. Filadelfo hesitated, a chill creeping up his spine, but the doors behind him thudded shut with a finality that left him no choice. He followed, each step feeling heavier than the last, as though he were descending into something far deeper than stone halls.

The letter from the Pope explained his new duties in meticulous detail. His role was simple: tend to the needs of a man kept beneath the Vatican—a man whose identity was never to be spoken of.

"Who is this?" asked a monk, his voice low and rasping as though it were unused to speaking. His gaze flicked to the hooded escort.

"Father Filadelfo," the escort replied. "He has been cleansed. He will not question his orders."

Filadelfo's mind felt clouded, his thoughts distant and blurred, as though someone had reached into his soul and swept away what didn't belong. Yet deep down, in the recesses of his being, something whispered that he was not free. Not truly.

The monk nodded, his eyes lingering on Filadelfo with something that felt uncomfortably close to pity. Then he turned and disappeared into the shadows.

The life he had known was gone. Now, he belonged to the Order of the Hidden Cross. His steps echoed down the stone corridor, the sound swallowed by the stillness around him. Somewhere in the silence, he thought he heard the faintest sound—a whisper, a breath, or the distant creak of something shifting beneath the earth. It was as though the monastery itself were alive, watching, waiting.

He clutched the letter tightly as he walked on, its weight far greater than its parchment. Whatever awaited him beneath the Vatican, he would never be the same again.

Chapter 17

Every Lock Has a Key

Joshua Carpenter's Journal – Entry 487:

"They say the truth has a way of slipping between the cracks of time. I've felt it, heard it, even seen it, rippling through the fabric of the worlds, but the truth itself remains elusive. Malleck is gone. The others, too. The Dark Matter holds them fast, unreachable, but not voiceless. I've learned this: Messages can pass where bodies cannot."

Joshua Carpenter sat cross-legged on the cold, cracked stone floor of the abandoned chapel, the silence pressing in around him like a vice. His fingers traced the ancient symbols drawn in chalk, the lines pulsing faintly in the flickering candlelight as if they breathed in time with his heartbeat. The air was thick with dust, the scent of ancient prayers mingling with a darker presence, something heavy and old. Even the saints depicted in the murals seemed to twist in the periphery of his vision, their eyes following him, judgmental and accusing. He could feel them watching, as they always did when he tampered with forces beyond his control.

But Joshua had grown accustomed to it, even if it still gnawed at the edges of his sanity. He had no choice.

"Let's hope this works," he muttered under his breath, adjusting one of the candles, its flame sputtering like a weak pulse. His hands shook slightly—not from fear, but from exhaustion. It had been years. Years of trying and failing. Years of incantations, rituals, and desperate attempts to bridge the gap between this world and the Dark Matter. The abyss where Malleck and the others were trapped.

His gaze flicked to the sigil on the floor, a precise combination of salt, crushed herbs, and sacred symbols. It buzzed with latent energy, a hum that he could feel in his bones. There had been failures before—many of them. But messages, he had learned, could cross the abyss. Words could pass where bodies couldn't. And that was all he needed. Just to get a message across.

The sigil pulsed beneath his hands, its energy biting at his skin like static. Joshua flinched, his concentration wavering. If he lost focus now, the fragile bridge would collapse, and with it, his one chance to reach Bussi.

Joshua inhaled deeply, the sharp metallic tang of magic filling his lungs, the power thrumming beneath the surface. His heart hammered in his chest, the weight of a thousand failed attempts pressing down on him. Every failure haunted him and whispered doubts into his mind. What if this doesn't work? What if they're lost forever? What if I'm already too late?

If the man beneath the Vatican was freed, it wouldn't just ripple through the multiverse—it would shatter it. Dimensions that once coexisted in fragile balance would collide, unravelling into chaos. And in that chaos, the Order would burn everything to keep their secret.

He shook the thoughts away, forcing himself to focus. Tonight was different. He had found something in the Hall of Memories, a place he had no right to access but had slipped into regardless. The Hall wasn't a physical place. It existed in the spaces between realities, guarded by the Memory Keepers, ancient beings who protected the knowledge of all things in all dimensions. But Joshua had been careful and had shielded himself from their gaze as he skimmed the ancient records, searching for the key.

And he had found it. A man, kept prisoner beneath the Vatican. A man who could change everything. He wasn't just any man—he was the only person in all the known dimensions to be singular, to exist as one, alone. There were a million versions of Joshua Carpenter and a million more of Bussi, or even his mother Zivah. Every person in every world had countless iterations. But not him. There was only one of this man, a man who was eternally the one being, untouched by the multiverse's endless web of possibilities. Singular, unduplicated. And that made him unique, special, dangerous even.

Joshua remembered what he'd seen in the Hall of Memories—the man's eyes, haunted by time, unyielding to the shifting realities around him. He was more than just a prisoner. His existence alone threatened to unravel the very fabric of every universe, every dimension. And if freed, the consequences would ripple out, touching every version of reality, splintering the fragile balance that had been kept for millennia.

"Beris," Joshua called softly, the name carrying a ripple of power through the air like a stone dropped into a still pond.

The shadows in the room twisted, coiling into a darker mass in the corner before slowly materialising into a small figure. Beris hovered just above the floor, his form flickering between solid and translucent, his glowing eyes shifting from gold to deep black with each blink. He was no larger than four inches tall, a being caught between worlds, never fully here or there.

"You called, my apprentice of doom?" Beris rasped, his voice like a dry whisper that echoed unnaturally in the small space. "Or was it more foolishness today? More attempts to save those who are already lost?"

Joshua's smirk was faint, but his voice carried a tremor of hope. "Not foolishness this time, I promise. I've got an idea."

Beris floated closer, crossing his tiny arms over his chest—barely more than flickers of shadow. "Ah, a new plan. You know, you should start numbering them. It'll be easier to remember which ones failed." His voice dripped with sarcasm.

Joshua's smirk faltered slightly. The failures weighed on him more than Beris knew. "I'm sending you on a little trip," he continued, his tone more serious now. "To deliver a message."

Beris' eyes narrowed. "Ah, messages. From saving souls to becoming the errand boy of the multiverse. What glorious descent." He paused, looking at Joshua more closely. "...Who is this message for?"

"A young priest," Joshua replied, kneeling to touch the sigil's lines. The hum of power beneath his fingertips sent a shiver down his spine. "His name is Bussi. He holds the key to unlocking everything."

Beris' sarcasm ceased as he hovered in the air, studying Joshua with an unreadable expression. "...Go on."

Joshua's hands trembled slightly as he stood, his heart thudding in his chest. Beris cocked his head. "The Order's watching him, aren't they? Poor priest. He has no idea what's waiting for him under that holy fortress."

Joshua's jaw tightened. "He doesn't need to. Not yet. Just tell him he holds the key. If he learns the truth, he'll know what to do. They'll kill him if they find out."

Beris chuckled, dark and throaty. "Ah yes, the Order. The Vatican's best-worst-kept secret. You do love your dangerous games, boy. This Order doesn't just kill—they erase. You're playing with fire."

"I know," Joshua whispered, the weight of it settling heavily in his bones. "But it has to be done. Bussi needs to know that he's part of something bigger than himself. If he learns the truth about the man they're holding beneath the Vatican, it could change everything. We're running out of time, Beris. You need to tell him."

Beris floated higher, his glowing eyes narrowing. "You're sending me into the Vatican's inner sanctum? And here I thought you had a shred of self-preservation left. But fine, I'll go. He connects to the Source when he meditates, doesn't he? That's how you'll get me through."

Beris hesitated, his flickering form still. "You're asking me to walk into a lion's den, Joshua. Do you know what the Order does to beings like me? They don't just erase—they make sure we never existed." His eyes, dark and uncertain, met Joshua's. "Are you sure about this?"

Joshua nodded, his throat tight with apprehension. "Wait! How do you know that?... never mind. Yes. That's the only time I can reach him without alerting the Order. I've slipped in and eavesdropped, but I can't deliver the message myself. It needs to be you because you're split between dimensions. They've been watching him too closely. We can't risk it any other way. You can enter his mind when he's meditating, and they won't be able to see or hear you two talking."

Beris circled the glowing sigil slowly, spinning idly. "And the message? What am I supposed to whisper in this holy man's ear?"

Joshua knelt by the sigil again, his fingers digging into the cool stone. The words came slowly, as if the weight of them was too much to bear. "Tell him he holds the key. That his curiosity will lead him to a truth so powerful it transcends time and space. But warn him—if the Order finds out, they'll kill him. They guard the man beneath the Vatican, and Bussi must uncover who that man is and free him. His role in this is more important than he realises."

Beris' eyes glinted with dark amusement. "Oh, a truth that transcends time and space. I love those. They always end so well for mortals." He floated closer to Joshua, twitching with anticipation. "And what of his fate? What should I say when he asks why he has been chosen?"

Joshua's voice dropped to a whisper, heavy with the knowledge he carried. "Tell him it's his destiny. That everything has led him to this moment. And when the time comes, he'll know what to do."

Beris hovered over the sigil, his gaze locked on Joshua's. "You're setting him on a dangerous path, Joshua. You know that once this begins, there's no stopping it."

"I know," Joshua replied, his voice barely audible. "But we have no choice."

With a click of his heels, Beris dissolved into the air, his tiny form vanishing into the shadows of the chapel, leaving behind only the faint hum of the ritual's power. Joshua watched him go, his body tense with the weight of what he had just set in motion. His breath came in short, ragged gasps, the exhaustion finally catching up to him.

Somewhere across the dimensions, a key was turning in a lock, a lock that had been sealed for millennia. And soon, the door to the Church's darkest secret would be opened.

Father Bussi sat cross-legged in his chamber, his breathing slow and deliberate as he sank deeper into meditation. The room around him seemed to dissolve, leaving only the pulsing thread of the Source, the divine connection that ran through all things. In this space, he felt closest to God, the great architect of the universe, as though the veil between the mortal and the divine had grown thin.

But tonight, something was wrong.

The peace he usually felt in this state was disrupted by a presence, something foreign creeping into his mind like a shadow stretching across the ground. At first, it was subtle, a faint whisper at the edges of his consciousness. But soon, it grew stronger, more tangible. It slithered into his thoughts, twisting them, pulling them in strange directions.

Then, the figure appeared.

Small, shadowy, with eyes that flickered between gold and black, its form barely solid in the haze of Bussi's meditative trance. The figure grinned, wide and unsettling, as it floated closer.

"Father Bussi," the voice rasped, cutting through the calm like a blade. "I bring you a message. From a boy named Joshua."

Bussi's heart stuttered in his chest. Joshua? He didn't know anyone personally by that name, and yet the sound of it stirred something deep within him, something ancient and familiar.

"Who… who are you?" Bussi's voice trembled, his mind struggling to maintain the peace he had cultivated.

"Shh, don't speak aloud," said Beris. "They will hear you. Speak with your mind, and you'll be safe."

"I am Beris," the figure replied, its voice a dark whisper in the recesses of his mind. "A messenger. Joshua sent me with a message. You hold the key, Father. The key to a truth so powerful, it has been hidden beneath the Vatican for centuries."

The peace Bussi had once felt shattered as the words sank in. His thoughts swirled, chaotic and unmoored, as the presence of Beris twisted the world around him. The room darkened, the air thickening like a weight pressing down on him.

"What truth?" Bussi's voice cracked, desperation creeping in. "What are you talking about?"

"The man they keep prisoner," Beris whispered, his form flickering in and out of existence. "You've felt it, haven't you? The pull? The whispers of something greater, something hidden. The Order of the Hidden Cross guards him. They've done so for millennia. But you, Father—you are the one who will unlock it all."

Bussi's mind reeled. He had heard rumours, whispers of the Order of the Hidden Cross, but no one spoke of it openly. The Vatican's best-kept secret. He had sensed something—always just out of reach—but now it felt as though the truth was clawing its way to the surface.

"Why me?" Bussi whispered, the weight of the revelation pressing down on him like a crashing wave.

"Because," Beris hissed, "this is your destiny. Everything has led you to this moment. And when the time comes, you will know what to do. But be careful, Father. The Order will kill you if they find out what you're seeking. They guard the man below, and they will stop at nothing to protect their secret."

Before Bussi could respond, the world around him fractured. The darkened chamber folded in on itself, collapsing into a void of swirling shadows. Beris' voice echoed through the chaos.

"Remember, Father, you hold the key. But don't let them know you're looking. Or you'll never leave the Vatican alive."

Joshua exhaled sharply, his body sagging under the weight of the ritual. The candles were nearly burned out, their flames flickering weakly in the oppressive darkness of the chapel. His limbs ached, and his mind throbbed with the strain of the spell, but it was done. The message had been delivered.

Beris was gone, sent to Bussi with a message that would either save him—or doom him. Joshua wasn't sure which.

Wiping the sweat from his brow, Joshua stood slowly, his legs unsteady beneath him. He had done everything he could. Now, all he could do was wait.

Somewhere across the infinite expanse of dimensions, a door had been unlocked. Soon, the Church's darkest secret would be revealed.

And when that happened, nothing would ever be the same again.

But as Joshua moved to snuff out the remaining candles, a tremor rippled through the air. It wasn't Beris or the lingering energy from the ritual—this was something else. The sigil on the floor, now faint and flickering, pulsed one final time before dimming entirely.

Father Bussi jolted awake, his heart pounding against his ribs, his breath coming in short, desperate gasps. The chamber was dark, the silence thick and oppressive. The familiar comfort of the Vatican's walls felt distant, as if the room itself were a prison, shrinking around him. The meditation had ended, but the echo of Beris' words still thrummed in his skull like the toll of a distant, mournful bell.

He had seen it. He had felt it.

The man beneath the Vatican.

His hands trembled as they fumbled to light the candle beside his bed. His fingers scraped against the cold metal of the matchbox, his movements awkward, betraying the panic racing through his veins. A flame finally sputtered to life, casting shaky shadows on the stone walls. But the faint light brought no comfort—only a stark reminder of the darkness that now haunted him.

The key. The truth. The man hidden beneath the Vatican for centuries.

Bussi sat up, clutching his chest as if to steady his hammering heart. His mind was a storm, torn between fear and a desperate need for answers. Beris had revealed just enough to ignite the flames of curiosity, but the truth now clawed at him relentlessly. He needed to know more. He had to know.

But why him? Why now? The whispers had always been there, faint and fleeting, but now they were deafening. Was this a test of his faith, or a punishment for his doubt?

But there was something else. A warning.

"They will kill you if they find out you're looking."

The words had slithered through his thoughts like a serpent, their cold promise sending chills through his spine. He rose to his feet, legs shaking, his robe clinging to his sweat-drenched body. He crossed to the small desk in the corner of his chamber, pulling out a worn leather-bound journal. He had to write it down—every word, every image, before it slipped away. His hand trembled as he scrawled the warnings Beris had given him:

"You hold the key, Father."

"They keep him prisoner beneath the Vatican."

"They will kill you if they know."

His pen scratched furiously across the page, but halfway through, he paused. The oppressive silence in the room felt unnatural. The shadows in the corners seemed to thicken, their edges blurring, shifting like living things.

Something is watching.

Bussi felt a chill crawl up his spine. He turned slowly, his breath shallow, scanning the room. The shadows seemed to shift and ripple in the candlelight. His pulse quickened.

"Who's there?" he whispered, barely able to force the words past the knot of fear tightening in his throat.

The air in the room grew colder. The shadows deepened.

And then, he heard it—a whisper. Faint, like a distant wind scraping across stone. It was soft at first, but it grew louder, more insistent, like hundreds of voices speaking at once, yet none of them clear. The sound filled the room, pressing in on him.

They know.

Bussi's breath caught in his throat. His eyes darted to the far corner of the room, where the darkness seemed to writhe like a living thing. His candle flickered violently, casting erratic shadows across the walls. He backed away from the desk, his heart racing, his body suddenly cold with terror.

The whispering intensified, the voices overlapping, forming a single, coherent thought.

They know.

Bussi stumbled backwards, knocking the chair over. His legs felt weak beneath him, his mind racing. He snatched up his rosary, gripping it tightly as he began to mutter a prayer under his breath. But the words came out broken, hollow. The prayer felt meaningless in the face of whatever presence had entered the room.

The shadows in the corner shifted again, and this time, they began to take shape. A figure emerged from the darkness—vaguely humanoid, but wrong. Its edges blurred, its form twisted, as if the shadows themselves were trying to break free. It stood tall, looming, its eyes—two burning, hollow orbs—fixed on Bussi.

He froze, clutching his rosary so tightly the beads bit into his skin. His back pressed against the cold stone wall, his breath shallow and ragged.

The figure didn't move. It simply watched him. Its presence was overwhelming, suffocating. The weight of it pressed down on him, filling the room with a cold, crushing dread.

Then, it spoke.

"You cannot hide from the Order, Father."

The voice was like ice, slicing through the air with a weight that left no room for argument. It was layered, like a thousand voices speaking in unison, yet none of them entirely human. Bussi's chest tightened.

"W-what do you want?" His voice trembled, barely a whisper.

The figure's head tilted slightly, its burning eyes narrowing. "The truth will break you. It will kill you."

The words pierced him like a knife. The truth. The man beneath the Vatican. The warnings Beris had given him surged back into his mind. The Order knew. They had always known. And now, they were watching him. But it wasn't just fear that gripped him now—there was something else. A fire burning in the pit of his stomach. Anger. Betrayal.

They had lied to him. The Church had hidden this from him—from everyone. All these years, he had served faithfully, blindly, and they had kept him in the dark. His faith wavered, but his resolve hardened.

"I won't stop," Bussi said, his voice shaking but defiant. "I need to know the truth. I need to know… who he is."

The figure remained silent, its eyes burning into him, its presence pressing down on him like a weight. Then, slowly, it began to dissipate, the shadows unravelling, curling into the air like smoke. But before it vanished entirely, its voice echoed once more through the chamber.

"If you seek the truth, you will find only death."

The shadows dissolved, leaving the room in a suffocating silence. Bussi collapsed to his knees, his body trembling, his breath coming in short, ragged gasps. The oppressive weight lifted, but the fear clung to him like a shroud.

He forced himself to stand, leaning heavily on the desk for support. His heart still pounded, but his mind was sharp now, focused. The Order knew. They were watching him. But that didn't matter anymore.

He had to find the man beneath the Vatican. And he had to do it before they could stop him.

Joshua sat cross-legged in the darkened chapel, staring into the dying embers of the last candle. His chest was tight, his muscles aching from the strain of the ritual. He could still feel the lingering energy in the air, the faint hum of power from the sigil now reduced to little more than a whisper.

He had pushed Bussi to the edge. Beris had played his part perfectly, weaving fear and paranoia into the fabric of Bussi's mind. The second incarnation—a shadow, a wraith made of fear and illusion—had delivered the final blow. They had broken Bussi just enough to make him diligent, to make him hide his actions, to make him desperate enough to act alone.

"Well," Beris appeared suddenly in the dim light, hovering just above the sigil. "He's sufficiently rattled. You were right—fear is quite the motivator for secrecy."

Joshua didn't respond immediately. His eyes were fixed on the flickering light, lost in thought. "It had to be done. If he's not careful, the Order will erase him like they've erased so many before him."

Beris floated lazily around the circle, his translucent body twitching. "You played it well. That little shadow incarnation of yours—impressive. Very convincing. He really believed it was the Order watching him."

Joshua exhaled slowly, his gaze still distant. "Fear keeps people quiet. Paranoia forces them into the shadows. If Bussi knows he's being watched—or thinks he is—he'll move carefully, quietly. It's the only way to keep him alive long enough to find the man."

Beris chuckled darkly. "Let's just hope he doesn't crack before he finds him. The way he was trembling? I thought he was going to lose his mind right there."

Joshua exhaled sharply. The shadow's presence had lingered longer than expected, but it had done its job. Bussi was rattled, just enough to keep him from trusting anyone but himself.

Joshua's expression tightened. "He's stronger than he looks. He has to be. We're too far in now. The Order won't stop if they catch wind of what he's doing. He's our only chance."

Beris cocked his head, watching Joshua intently. "You say 'chance' like this is all still under control."

Joshua's jaw clenched, his hand tightening around the edge of his robe. "It is. For now."

But Beris wasn't convinced. His eyes flickered as he floated in lazy circles. "You're playing with fire, Joshua. The Order is dangerous, but what you've done to Bussi—there's a thin line between paranoia and madness. What if he goes too far? What if he turns on us?"

Joshua's eyes darkened. "He won't. He can't. The truth is too important for him to turn back now. He needs to find the man beneath the Vatican—before the Order silences him for good."

Beris hovered closer, his voice dropping to a conspiratorial whisper. "And if he doesn't?"

Joshua didn't answer. The question lingered in the air, heavy and unspoken.

They both knew the stakes were too high for failure.

Joshua froze, his hand hovering above the last candle.

Then he felt it—a pull. A force, subtle at first, like the faintest tug at the edge of his mind. But it grew stronger, sharper, like fingers dragging him toward the centre of the circle. His breath caught in his throat as the chapel walls seemed to darken, the candlelight shrinking into tiny pinpricks of fire swallowed by the abyss.

For a moment, just a heartbeat, Joshua thought he saw something. In the farthest corner of his vision, where the shadows clung the thickest, a figure moved. It wasn't Beris. It was taller. More solid. Its presence was suffocating and oppressive, like the weight of the Dark Matter itself.

Joshua's chest tightened. He knew, without understanding why, that the message had reached more than just Bussi.

A tremor rippled through the sigil at his feet, a pulse that made the floor vibrate. Joshua's hands began to shake. This wasn't right. The ritual was never meant to open this door—only to send a message. Yet something—someone—had crossed over.

The scent wrapped around him, sickly sweet and hauntingly familiar. His mother's perfume. But she had died years ago—hadn't she? The figure moved closer, its shadow stretching toward him, and Joshua swore he heard her voice, soft and broken, whispering his name. What if it's not her? What if something is wanting me to think t's her to draw me out?

He swallowed hard, his pulse pounding in his ears. This wasn't supposed to happen. The ritual wasn't meant to open this door. But now, it was too late. Whatever lay beyond the veil—whatever watched him now—had already crossed the threshold.

And it was waiting.

Chapter 18

The Shadow's Deception

It was late in the evening, and Zivah and Asher sat together in her family's tent, the air thick with the scent of evening spices and the soft glow of oil lamps reflecting off richly woven tapestries. The warmth of the day lingered, but it only added to the heaviness between them. Asher tried to meet Zivah's eyes, smiling, teasing her in an effort to break the unease that seemed to radiate from her every movement.

"You know," he said, voice light but edged with nervous energy, "sometimes I still can't believe we're getting married. There was a time I thought I'd be sent off to become a priest—imagine that!" He chuckled, leaning closer, the warmth of his presence an unspoken reassurance. "You saved me, Zivah. You saved me from that path, and I'll be forever grateful. I can't wait to be with you. Truly."

Zivah's hands stilled, and her eyes, once distant, snapped back to meet his. There was no mirth there, no relief. Instead, there was a flicker of fear—of panic—as if his words had triggered something she could no longer hold back. "Asher..." Her voice wavered, and the calm he tried to create shattered in an instant. "Asher... I'm pregnant."

Asher's smile faded as if stolen from his face. His breath hitched, heart pounding in his chest. "How?" The word felt stupid and insufficient, and it tumbled out of his mouth without thought. They had been waiting—saving themselves for their wedding night, which was only weeks away.

Zivah's eyes brimmed with tears, and she shook her head, the silver clasp in her hair trembling with her. "I don't know how it happened. I... I had a dream, a dream so vivid, so real..." Her voice broke as she recounted the night she was overtaken by something, or someone, in her sleep. "I thought it was just a dream, but... but then my body changed, and I knew it couldn't have been just that." Her voice was barely more than a whisper. "I know how it sounds, Asher. I know you won't believe me, but I swear, it was no one else. I would never..."

Asher's world tilted and spun. His thoughts fractured and crumbled like a vase dropped from a great height, shattering on impact. He searched Zivah's eyes, desperate for some clue that this was all a mistake, a misunderstanding—but all he saw was sincerity and fear. His mind screamed at the impossibility, but his heart—his heart still ached for her, the woman he loved beyond all things. He wanted to believe her, to wrap her in his arms and protect her from whatever terror she faced. But the doubt... it gnawed at him like an unseen rat, burrowing deeper with every word she spoke.

He tried to speak, but his voice cracked with the weight of disbelief. "How can I know this is true?" The words came out sharp, cutting through the fragile thread of composure they shared. He didn't want to hurt her, didn't want to accuse her—but how could he reconcile this? Was this dream an elaborate story to cover a betrayal? How could he trust a vision, a nightmare, over the reality they shared?

Unable to make sense of the storm inside him, Asher abruptly stood. The silence that followed was a terrible, fragile thing. Zivah reached out, fingers trembling, but her voice faltered, and the tears that had gathered in her eyes spilled down her cheeks. She did not plead, did not beg, but her look was an agony of unspoken desperation. But he couldn't face her—not like this. He turned and walked out of the tent into the cool night air, leaving behind the only woman he had ever truly loved. That night, Asher returned to his family's tent, and from that moment on, he did not speak to Zivah again.

In the days that followed, the shadows of doubt and rage tangled around Asher's thoughts. He could find no peace. Every fleeting memory of Zivah, every shared smile and whisper of love, was now tainted with the ghost of her confession. The story she told— the dream that left her with child—was absurd, impossible, and yet it was there, lurking at the edges of his thoughts like a serpent ready to strike. What if... what if it were true? What did that mean for him, for them, for the life they had promised to build together?

Asher couldn't bear it. Each day felt like a battle between the love he bore for Zivah and the creeping suspicion that clung to him like oil he couldn't wash away.

One moonless night, as he sat outside his family's tent by the fire pit, staring into the erratic dance of the flames, a chill wrapped around him, unnatural and biting. He rubbed his arms, glancing around uneasily. At first, it seemed like a trick of the firelight—a flicker of movement at the edge of his vision, a shadow twisting in a way that defied the natural world. Asher's heart pounded. He turned to leave when a voice, smooth as silk and dark as poisoned honey, whispered from the edge of the darkness.

"Aashher."

He froze, turning slowly. "Who's there?" he called, but the firelight revealed nothing but empty night. A shadow shifted again, dancing at the edge of the fire's glow, twisting and reshaping itself into a figure cloaked in darkness so deep it swallowed the light around it.

The figure's outline was only vaguely human, but it was the eyes—eyes that glimmered like cold steel in the dark—that gripped him with a fear he had never known.

"I am... a friend," the figure spoke, its voice calm and almost soothing, a voice that slithered into his thoughts like an unwelcome guest. "I know what troubles you. I know the pain in your heart, Asher."

Asher's fists clenched, the veins in his neck tightening. "What do you know of my pain?" he spat, but his voice betrayed him; it trembled.

The figure stepped closer, the darkness around him swirling like a living cloak. "The child that Zivah carries... is not yours."

Anger flared hot in Asher's chest. He took a step toward the figure, wanting to strike out, to force the shadow to retreat, but his hands fell limp by his sides. "How do you know that? How could you possibly know what happened?"

The figure's voice lowered to a silken whisper, a comforting lie wrapped in poison. "Because I have seen what you have not. Not all dreams are harmless, Asher. Some dreams take root, twisting themselves into the waking world in ways we cannot understand. But there is a way to know the truth... to uncover the deception."

Asher felt trapped, desperate. The words clawed at him like a thorn bush, entangling his thoughts. "What do you want me to do?" he demanded, voice shaking. "How do I... how do I find out?"

"You must go to the forest," the figure said, leaning in so close that Asher felt the icy chill of its breath on his face. "Seek out the shaman who lives beyond the mountains. He alone has the power to see through lies, to reveal what has truly happened."

"I don't... I don't understand," Asher stammered, the shadows seeming to creep closer around him, tightening. "You expect me to believe you? Why should I trust anything you say?" He wanted to sound resolute, to reclaim control, but the fear laced his voice like venom.

A low, sinister chuckle emanated from the figure, a sound that seemed to come from everywhere and nowhere. "I do not ask you to trust me blindly. Trust the doubt in your own heart, Asher. Trust the unease that gnaws at you when you think of the child." The figure's voice coiled around him, seductive, sinister. "Tell me—do you not feel that something is amiss? That there is more to Zivah's story than what she has told you?"

Asher's throat tightened. The figure's words were a knife to his soul, cutting deep into the doubts he had tried to bury. He could not deny it—the questions, the confusion. "What do you want from me?" His voice was barely more than a whisper.

"What I want is what you want, Asher—the truth. Zivah is hiding something from you, and you deserve to know. You loved her, didn't you?" The figure's voice softened, coaxing. "Or perhaps... you still do."

"Of course I do!" Asher's shout tore through the stillness. "I love her more than anything! That's why... that's why this hurts so much."

"Precisely," the figure whispered, and though its face was hidden in shadow, Asher could almost sense a smile forming. "If you love her, you must face the truth, no matter how bitter it may be. I am offering you a way to lift the veil of lies that clouds your mind."

Asher stepped closer, his face inches from the darkness. "Why help me? What's in it for you? Why do you care about me, about Zivah?"

For a moment, there was silence as the figure weighed its words carefully. "Once, I, too, was a man deceived. A man who lost everything because I did not see clearly. I have seen the pain that lies can cause, Asher. I would not wish that fate upon you."

"And... if I go?" Asher asked finally, voice trembling. "If I find this shaman... will he truly show me what happened to Zivah?"

The figure leaned even closer, its presence like a cold wind wrapping around Asher's soul. "The shaman sees beyond what others cannot. He will reveal to you what is hidden, strip away all deceit. But you must be prepared, Asher. The truth is often a bitter thing. It can cut deeper than any blade."

Asher's eyes dropped to the ground, thoughts spinning like a storm. "I can't just leave," he said, his voice barely audible. "My family... Zivah..."

"Sometimes, to protect those we love, sacrifices must be made," the figure said, its voice like a whisper from the depths of the abyss. "This journey could save Zivah from a pain she has not yet felt. When you return, the path will be clear. You will know what must be done."

"But what if the truth... what if it's worse than I can bear?"

"Then you will be stronger for it," the figure replied darkly. "The shaman will reveal what has been hidden and show you the path only you can walk." The shadow man started to dissipate while saying, "Whatever you find, Asher, you will be free—free from the chains of uncertainty that bind you now."

Asher now sat alone outside his family's tent, staring at the dying embers of the fire pit. Every flicker of the flames seemed to pull him deeper into his thoughts, thoughts that had grown darker and more tangled with each passing day. He tried to make sense of Zivah's words, of the dream she claimed had left her with child, but every explanation seemed to unravel like loose threads in his hands. How could something like this happen? How could a dream carry flesh and blood into the world?

A few nights later, everyone had retired for the night, leaving Asher in a heavy silence that only served to amplify his fears. He dropped his head into his hands, wrestling with the storm raging inside his heart—the anger, the doubt, the love that refused to let go.

The cool night air felt sharp against his skin, and just when Asher thought he might suffocate under the weight of his own thoughts, he felt it: a coldness that settled over him, creeping into his bones like a shadow.

"Asher."

The voice was unmistakable—the same voice that had whispered to him a few nights before, leading him into darkness. Asher's eyes snapped open, and there, standing just beyond the circle of the dying fire, was the shadow figure.

"You again," Asher muttered, clenching his fists to stop his hands from trembling. He rose to his feet, his voice low and edged with fear. "What do you want from me? Why won't you leave me alone?"

The shadow figure's form twisted slightly, the darkness around him deepening until his outline blurred as though he were part of the very night itself. "I come to offer you what you seek—truth," the figure whispered, his voice smooth, almost kind. "You must leave, Asher. Find the shaman, and all will become clear."

Asher's face tightened with anger and desperation. "And what then? You expect me to just walk away from everything—my family, Zivah? They'll question why I'm gone! My family will think I've abandoned them, and Zivah... she'll think I've left her for good. How can you ask me to do this?"

The shadow figure's voice was steady, unyielding. "You know that you cannot stay. Not like this. You cannot raise a child that is not yours, nor can you live with the burden of doubt that eats away at your heart."

"Doubt?" Asher spat, taking a step closer. "You've planted that doubt. Before you, I never—"

"Before me, you were already doubting, Asher," the figure interrupted smoothly. "I only spoke the words that you dared not say aloud. Tell me... when Zivah confessed to you, when she told you of her dream—did you truly believe her? Or was there a voice inside of you, a voice that whispered 'Lies'?"

Asher's jaw clenched, and he looked away, unable to meet the figure's eyes. He wanted to deny it, to shout that Zivah had never lied to him before. But in the depths of his heart, the truth clawed its way to the surface. He had doubted her. Even as he tried to comfort her, to believe her story, a part of him had screamed that none of it made sense. That she was hiding something.

The figure's voice softened, almost coaxing. "You must know the truth. Not just for yourself, but for Zivah—for the life you would build together. Do you truly wish to bind yourself to lies? Or would you rather face the truth, no matter how dark?"

Asher's face twisted in pain as the weight of his choices pressed down on him. "And what about my family?" he whispered. "If I leave now, without any explanation... they'll think I've gone mad. They'll never understand."

"Your family will grieve," the figure said, the words rolling off his tongue like a prophecy, "but they will forgive. You are not abandoning them, Asher—you are protecting them. And you are protecting yourself. This path is not an easy one, but it is the only way to make sense of what has been hidden from you."

"But Zivah..." Asher's voice broke, the love he still held for her clinging to his every word. "What will she think? She'll believe I've forsaken her. She'll hate me."

The figure drew closer, his form still obscured in shadow, but the faint glimmer of his eyes piercing through the darkness. "Zivah will understand in time. And if she truly loves you as you love her, then she will wait. When you return, all will be made right. The lies will fall away like leaves, and the truth will bloom between you. But only if you go now."

A silence hung between them, heavy and filled with unspoken fears. Asher could hear his own breathing, could feel his heart pounding in his chest like a drum. What would become of him if he left? Would he ever be able to return? He looked toward the flap of the tent, toward the camp that lay beyond—the people he'd leave behind, the life that was slowly crumbling around him.

"And if I don't go?" Asher asked finally, his voice barely louder than a whisper. "What if I stay?"

"Then you will never know," the figure said, his voice darkening like a storm cloud rolling over the horizon. "You will live a life shrouded in shadows, tied to a child that is not your own, a future built on a foundation of lies. But you already know this. Deep down, you have always known. You cannot unsee what has been revealed."

Asher closed his eyes, the truth of those words seeping into him like poison. The figure's voice, the doubts he carried, the confusion that tore at his heart—it was all too much. He needed to know, to see clearly. And if this journey, this one journey, was the only way to uncover what had happened, then he had no choice.

The figure seemed to sense his resolve and stepped back, the shadows around him swirling like tendrils of smoke. "Follow the moon until it begins to wane. Cross three rivers and find the path where the trees grow so dense that no sunlight touches the earth. There, the shaman waits. And when you find him, he will know why you have come."

Asher looked down at his feet, his mind racing through the consequences of this decision. It felt as though he was standing on the edge of a cliff, and before him lay a drop into the unknown. But he could not live like this. He could not bear the torment of doubt any longer.

"All right," he said at last, his voice cracking with the weight of it. "I'll go."

The shadow figure's form seemed to swell with approval, and for a moment, Asher could almost swear that he saw a smile—a glimmer of satisfaction flickering in the darkness. "Good," the figure murmured, his voice like a breeze that chills the soul. "The truth will set you free, Asher. And when you return, you will know what must be done."

And then, as quickly as he had appeared, the shadow figure faded away, leaving Asher standing alone in the cold, empty silence of the night.

Asher's decision was not made easily, but when dawn broke, he was ready. With the shadows of his past trailing behind him like a curse, he left the camp without a word. The voice of the shadow figure still echoed in his ears, cold and clear: "For Zivah... for the truth... for the child."

The night cloaked Asher as he made his way out of the camp, the soft murmur of the sleeping village behind him fading into silence. He could not afford to think about Zivah, to think about the grief in her eyes when he left her, or the unanswered questions his absence would stir in his family. Those thoughts were daggers, and if he let them cut too deep, he might lose his resolve. With every step he took, the shadow figure's words filled his mind like a drumbeat: "For Zivah... for the truth... for the child." He repeated the words like a mantra, trying to will away the doubts that clawed at his sanity. He needed to find this shaman. He needed answers.

The figure's directions rang in his mind, haunting and strange: Follow the moon until it wanes, cross three rivers, and seek the place where no sunlight touches the ground.

He hesitated at the edge of the camp, turning back one last time to look at the tent where Zivah lay. His heart clenched painfully as he imagined her waking to find him gone. Could he truly leave her? Would she ever understand why? Yet the shadow's words gnawed at his mind: You must know the truth. Trust the doubt in your heart. The weight of that doubt crushed him as he took his first step into the night.

The first night, Asher walked until the world around him seemed like a blur, moving as though in a fevered dream. The moon hung heavy in the sky, and he followed it as if tethered to its glow, never looking back. As the days passed, the landscape changed. Trees twisted into unrecognisable shapes, their branches hanging like skeletal hands reaching down to claw at him as he moved.

The forest seemed alive, its gnarled branches reaching like skeletal hands, the brambles tangling his legs as though urging him to turn back. The air grew heavier with each step, carrying whispers he dared not follow. And when he slept—when exhaustion forced him to rest for a few hours at a time—the dreams came.

Dreams of darkness. Dreams of a shadow figure with eyes like polished stone, watching him from the edge of the firelight. And dreams of Zivah, her voice calling out to him from somewhere far away, echoing through endless tunnels of black. But every time he reached for her, she was swallowed by the dark, and he would awaken with a start, sweat-soaked and trembling.

After crossing the third river, Asher entered a part of the forest that felt different—older, as if it had stood for centuries without the touch of man. The trees grew so close together that they formed a thick canopy above, blotting out the sky. And here, he felt it—a presence, a watchful silence that hung around him like a shroud. He trudged through the underbrush until he could go no further, and then he saw it—a clearing ahead, like an eye of calm in a sea of madness.

In the centre of the clearing stood the cottage. Small, crooked, and weathered, it looked like it had sprouted from the earth itself, the moss and vines clinging to its wooden frame like flesh to bone. Smoke drifted from the chimney, spiralling upward into the darkness. Asher felt a shiver of foreboding, but he had come too far to turn back now.

The cottage crouched in the clearing, its moss-covered frame blending with the forest as though it had always been there. Smoke curled lazily from the chimney, and the air seemed to hold its breath as Asher approached.

Each step felt like a descent into some unknown pit. Before he could knock, the door swung open as if pulled by invisible hands, revealing a dimly lit interior. There stood an old man, bent with age, but his eyes—those eyes were sharp, too sharp, cutting into Asher like blades. The shaman wore a cloak of deep red, frayed at the edges, and around his neck hung a cord strung with bones and feathers that rattled softly as he moved.

"Asher," the shaman said in a voice that was both a whisper and a growl, as if he spoke from somewhere deep below the earth. "I have been expecting you."

Asher faltered on the threshold, his hand trembling as it hovered over the doorframe. "How do you know my name?" His voice came out hoarse and cracked, sounding like it belonged to someone else.

The shaman's lips curled into a smile, revealing yellowed teeth. "I know many things," he replied with an unnerving calm that seemed to still the very air around them. "Come inside. Sit with me. I will brew you a tea... and all will become clear."

Hesitant but desperate for answers, Asher stepped inside, the warmth of the cottage wrapping around him like a suffocating blanket. The walls were lined with jars and dried plants, roots and powders of colours he'd never seen before. The smell was over-whelming—a mix of herbs, incense, and something far more pun-gent, like the rotting bark of a dead tree. In the centre of the room, a low-burning hearth cast flickering shadows across the wooden floor, making them dance like tortured souls.

The shaman gestured toward a rough wooden stool by the hearth, and Asher sat down, his muscles taut with tension. The shaman snapped his fingers, and without warning, a porcelain cup floated from a nearby shelf, borne by unseen hands. It came to rest before Asher, and steam curled upward from the tea, carrying with it a scent both sweet and earthy. Asher stared, his eyes wide, at the floating cup, disbelief mixing with a childlike wonder. His instincts screamed at him to run, to leave this cursed place, but something else—a compulsion he could not explain—kept him there.

"Drink," the shaman said softly, his voice a lullaby of venom. "It will calm your spirit... and open your mind to what you must see."

Asher's hands shook as he lifted the cup to his lips. The tea was warm, and as it flowed down his throat, a strange, intoxicating calm washed over him, clouding the sharp edges of his thoughts. It felt like sinking into a warm bath after a brutal storm, and for the first time in days, he felt... at peace. But the peace was fragile, too delicate, and he could feel a dark undercurrent pulling him deeper.

"I don't understand," Asher mumbled, his vision beginning to blur at the edges. "Zivah... the child... how..."

The shaman's eyes burned like twin embers, and he leaned closer, so close that Asher could smell the decay on his breath. "The child is not yours, Asher," the shaman hissed, his voice rising above the crackle of the hearth. "But the truth is hidden, buried deep. To see clearly, we must cleanse your mind."

And then the chanting began—an ancient, guttural language that twisted the air around them like a snake coiling around its prey. Each word seemed to burrow into Asher's thoughts, clawing away at his memories, tearing them apart like paper in the wind. The flames of the hearth flared, turning from orange to a sickly green, and shadows writhed on the walls, taking on forms that defied reason—twisting limbs, fanged faces, slithering tendrils.

Asher's limbs grew heavy, numbness spreading like poison through his veins. His vision darkened, the world dissolving into smears of colour and shapes. He tried to hold onto the last threads of his memories—Zivah's face, the warmth of her hand, the sound of her voice—but they slipped away, swallowed by the darkness and the shaman's voice, which drummed louder and louder until it was the only thing left.

When he awoke, it was as if he had slept for a thousand years. The chanting had ceased, and the cottage around him felt dreamlike, unreal. A fog hung over his mind, dulling his senses and clouding his thoughts. The shaman's face loomed above him, triumphant, his eyes gleaming like wet stone.

"Now, Asher," the shaman said, his voice thick with malice, "you must find Joshua. He is a danger to all that you hold dear. Seek him out... and end him."

Asher, now afraid, got up and stumbled from the cottage, the cold air biting into his lungs as he gasped for breath. The path ahead seemed endless, twisting into darkness, and he walked as though in a trance, driven by a compulsion he could not fight. But the forest, once a place of stillness, seemed to awaken around him. The branches creaked like bones, and the shadows seemed to stalk him, moving just beyond the edge of sight.

Asher wandered through the forest, the night clinging to him like a wet shroud. The path twisted and turned in ways that made no sense, as though the very trees conspired to lead him astray. His thoughts were clouded, his purpose blurred; only fragments remained—visions of a face he couldn't recall, a child named Joshua he was meant to find. The journey felt endless, each step heavier than the last as if he were walking through a dream he couldn't wake from.

It was then that he saw the glimmer of firelight through the branches—a small, flickering warmth against the endless black. Drawn to it like a moth, Asher pushed through the brambles, the thorns scraping his arms and tearing his clothes. He stumbled into a small clearing where a man sat by a fire, a cooking pot hanging over the flames, the savoury scent of roasted meat filling the night air.

The man looked up as Asher approached, his face half-lit by the fire's glow—a rugged, worn face, but not unkind. He had sharp eyes, eyes that seemed to take in everything at once, yet his expression held an odd, almost practised calm.

"Welcome, traveller," the man said, his voice warm but laced with something unreadable. He gestured to the empty space across the fire. "Come. You must be tired. Sit. Share my fire."

Asher felt a strange compulsion to obey, the words settling into his bones like an enchantment. He nodded, feeling a heaviness in his limbs as he moved toward the fire, sitting down on the rough ground. The heat of the flames was comforting against the cold of the forest night, and Asher found himself relaxing, if only for a moment.

"I... thank you," he managed to say, his voice low and unsure. The firelight cast long shadows across the man's face, making his eyes seem to gleam in the darkness. "I... I've been travelling for..."

His voice trailed off as he tried to remember how long it had been, but the days had bled into one another, an endless journey with no clear beginning or end. And then, there was the other matter—the gnawing realisation that he couldn't remember why he had been travelling in the first place. He opened his mouth to speak again, but a stab of pain shot through his skull, cutting off his words.

The man watched him closely, his eyes narrowing with what might have been pity—or might have been something else entirely. "You seem lost, friend," he said, leaning forward to ladle stew from the pot into a wooden bowl. "And weary, no doubt. What brings you out into this darkness?"

"I'm... looking for someone," Asher murmured, trying to pull the threads of his memory together, but they unravelled as soon as he touched them. "Someone... important." He faltered, the name slipping away from him like water through his fingers. "My name is... my name..." He gripped his head in his hands, frustration and panic clawing at his insides. Why couldn't he remember his name? Why did everything feel so distant, so dreamlike?

The man's smile widened, though it did not reach his eyes. "Do not worry," he said gently. "The forest plays tricks on the mind, steals away what is precious to us. But sit, eat, and let the fire warm your bones. All will come back to you in time."

Asher nodded numbly, taking the bowl of stew that the man offered. He hadn't realised how hungry he was until the first spoonful hit his tongue—the rich flavours exploded in his mouth, and he ate greedily, the warmth of the food easing the chill that had settled in his bones. The man watched him as he ate, his gaze unwavering as if studying Asher for something unseen.

"You're kind," Asher said through mouthfuls of stew, feeling a deep, aching gratitude he couldn't quite explain. "I... I've been so lost... so... alone." He couldn't remember the last time he'd shared a fire with someone, couldn't remember... anything, really. Just the forest, and the moon, and..."

"You are safe now," the man said, his voice low and soothing. "Eat. Rest. Let the darkness fall away."

For a time, they sat in silence, the crackling of the fire the only sound that filled the night. The man occasionally stirred the pot, a soft smile playing on his lips as Asher ate. And yet, there was something about the way the man moved—the measured grace of his gestures, the way his eyes never wavered from Asher—that set the hairs on the back of Asher's neck standing on end.

Asher finished his bowl, the food sitting heavy in his stomach. He felt... dazed, disoriented. His eyes drooped, the world around him blurring as if the very air had thickened into a fog. He rubbed his temples, trying to focus, but the man's voice seemed to echo through his skull, making it difficult to think.

"You should rest," the man said, and there was an edge to his voice now—a sharpness that hadn't been there before. He rose to his feet, moving to Asher's side. "The night is long, and the forest unforgiving. But you have nothing to fear, not while I'm here."

Asher tried to respond, tried to thank him, but the words tangled on his tongue. He was so tired, the pull of sleep stronger than any force he had ever known. The world spun around him, and he clutched at his stomach, a dull ache spreading through his core.

And then, it all happened too fast.

The man moved like a flash, one moment standing beside the fire, the next standing over Asher, a knife in his hand—a blade thin and wickedly sharp. Before Asher could react, before he could cry out, the man plunged the knife deep into his belly, the blade sliding between his ribs with a sickening ease.

The pain was instant and overwhelming, a searing agony that tore through Asher like wildfire. His mouth opened in a scream that never came, only a strangled gasp as the breath was forced from his lungs. He tried to scramble backward, but his body was slow and unresponsive, and all he managed to do was press his back against the hard, unforgiving earth.

The man was unrelenting, his face twisting into a grimace of concentration as he drove the knife upward, slicing through flesh and muscle in a single, brutal motion. The blade carved its way to Asher's sternum, and with a wet, tearing sound, his torso opened like a gutted animal, blood spilling over his lap, steaming in the night air.

Asher's eyes were wide, wild with terror, his hands instinctively moving to clutch at the gaping wound, trying to hold in the insides that now spilled out between his fingers. But the man was merciless, pushing Asher's hands aside as though he were peeling back the layers of a ripe fruit, the blade glistening red in the firelight.

"Please... please..." Asher croaked, blood pooling in his mouth, but the man did not stop. With a grim finality, the man plunged his hand into the wound, his fingers wrapping around Asher's intestines. And then, with a sickening, twisting yank, he pulled—hard—and Asher felt his guts spill out of him in a single, agonising motion.

The world became pain—endless, unimaginable pain—as Asher's innards slithered out of his body like serpents, falling in a steaming heap on the ground before him. The smell of iron and rot filled the air, a stench so overpowering it made his head swim. He tried to scream, but only blood bubbled from his lips, dribbling down his chin in crimson rivers.

The man looked down at him, holding Asher's entrails in his blood-soaked hands, and his smile returned—cold, cruel, and devoid of any humanity. "I can't have you going back to kill Joshua," he whispered, his voice barely more than a breath against Asher's ear. "The shaman's spell bound you, but this forest will be your grave. The earth will consume you, your bones never found."

Asher's vision swam, darkness closing in at the edges as his blood poured out onto the forest floor. He felt cold—so very, very cold—and his limbs went numb, the pain fading to a distant throb as his strength left him. He tried to say something—to ask why, to curse the man, to do something—but his mouth could form no words, only a soft, rasping breath.

The man tossed Asher's intestines aside, letting them hit the ground with a sickening splat. He watched as Asher's eyes fluttered, watched the life drain from them until they were only hollow, staring things, reflecting the firelight one last time before closing forever.

Asher's body went limp, the last shuddering breath escaping him in a wet gurgle. The man stood, wiping the blood from his hands onto his robes, his eyes flickering like embers in the dying fire. And as Asher's blood seeped into the earth, the ground around him seemed to shift—roots and vines snaking over his body, pulling him into the soil, burying him beneath the earth.

The forest swallowed Asher like a beast reclaiming its prey, the soil shifting as roots coiled around his limbs, dragging him down into the cold, dark depths. The ground beneath the man's feet quivered, a slow, almost deliberate movement as if the forest itself were savouring this moment—this fresh offering of blood and flesh. Soon, all that remained of Asher was a tangle of displaced leaves and disturbed earth, his body pulled deep below where no sunlight would ever touch.

The man stood over the spot, his expression unreadable as he watched the forest finish its gruesome work. For a long moment, there was only silence—the kind that presses against the eardrums like a weight, that hums with a tension too thick to break. He breathed in deeply, the scent of fresh blood mixing with the earthy decay of the forest floor.

Then, he spoke—a single, low murmur, his voice barely louder than the whispering wind. "Sleep now, lost one. The forest will cradle you as you fade into nothing."

The fire crackled, its flames licking upward in defiance of the night, throwing dancing shadows that seemed to pulse with life. The man stepped back from the fresh grave, his eyes dark and empty as twin voids. He cleaned the blade slowly, methodically, wiping the gore away until the metal gleamed silver again, sharp as moonlight on water.

With a final glance at the place where Asher's body had been swallowed, the man turned to walk away, leaving the fire to burn down to embers, he himself wisping into a fog and dispersing into the tree canopy, up to the moonlight, and gone out of sight.

As the man faded into the shadows, a faint shimmer caught the corner of his eye—a trace of energy, like a tear in the fabric of the world. He paused, the glimmer pulling at his thoughts like an unfinished thread. The shaman's spell had bound Asher's will, but its ripple had reached farther than intended. Somewhere, far from this cursed forest, Joshua stirred, unaware of the shadow that now stretched toward him.

The forest settled back into its rhythm—trees swaying in the wind, the rustle of leaves a soft and haunting lullaby. But beneath the earth, where no one could see, Asher's body lay broken and twisted, buried in a grave of roots and thorns, consumed by the very forest that had led him to his end.

And as the night grew deeper and the fire finally flickered out, the darkness seemed to thicken—an oppressive shroud that blanketed the world. Somewhere in the distance, a low, guttural laugh echoed through the trees as if the forest itself were amused by the events that had transpired, revelling in the torment it had borne witness to.

There would be no morning for Asher, no answers to the questions that had plagued him. The shadowy figure that had sent him on this path would remain a mystery, the truth of Zivah's child forever buried with him beneath the earth. And in the forest, where ancient secrets whispered through the branches and where blood and soil mixed like old lovers, the cycle of lies and darkness continued uninterrupted.

In the cold, still silence of the woods, all that remained was the distant memory of a man who had sought the truth and found only death—a truth more bitter than any blade and a death as cruel as the night itself.

Chapter 19

The Whisper in the Dark

The Master of Shadows watched from the darkness. He was always watching. It was his curse, his duty—to witness the rise and fall of countless worlds. Few spoke his name, but those who glimpsed his form knew him as a being woven from shadow and silence. Uriel was not simply one shadow among many—he was the Shadow Watcher, first among the Memory Keepers, once the loyal servant of the Nameless Gods who formed the multiverse from the empty void eons ago. But over time, Uriel became more than their servant; he became their betrayer.

The old gods had designed Uriel to oversee the endless web of life and death that made up the multiverse. He was the keeper of all memory, the one who saw and knew all things that existed. For eons, he carried out his duties—watching, recording, and guiding events from the shadows, all to maintain the cycle of life, suffering, and death. Each soul that existed was but a thread spun from an infinite loom, endlessly replicated in every possible reality. Until him.

Uriel had come across countless souls, each one with a billion versions across the endless branches of the multiverse. But Yehoshua was different—he was not bound to any variation or alternate form. There were not endless versions of Yehoshua across the myriad of worlds; there was only one. Singular, distinct, and unbound. The gods were afraid of this singularity. A being who existed outside their rules threatened their intricate cycle—the endless loop of creation, suffering, and destruction they played for their amusement, like a young boy getting his amusement from plucking wings off insects or using a magnifying glass to laser bean ants. Unlike every other creature they had spun into existence, Yehoshua stood apart. He alone saw through the design, saw the chains hidden in the shadows, and he sought to break them.

When Yehoshua came to Earth, the gods were quick to recognize his threat. His power defied human limits, his purpose defied their control, and he was too strong to be silenced. For years, they tried to kill him. Torture, poison, spells, weapons—none of it could destroy him. Death itself was a stranger to him. And so, in desperation, the powers that feared him found another way to subdue him. Saul, a zealous man with radical ideas and dreams of world domination, sought to imprison Yehoshua. Under Saul's direction, Yehoshua was drugged, bound in chains forged with forgotten spells, and hidden away deep underground, entombed beneath layers of magic that no human could break. The world was made to forget him, his presence and defiance erased from the threads of reality. Only the legacy that Saul or was it now Paul told the people it was.

The old gods granted Uriel the role of Master Memory Keeper—a collector and guardian of every thought, every moment across the countless worlds. He could see lives unfold, memories form, and secrets deepen across the vastness of existence. But the day Yehoshua was imprisoned, Uriel felt a ripple he had never experienced before—a rupture in the weave of the multiverse. He sensed a presence, a singular mind, and a defiance that the gods had long sought to conceal. Uriel became aware of Yehoshua as if awakening from a deep slumber. He sensed a purity that rebelled against the gods' cruelty—a clarity of purpose that stood against the endless pain and death they had orchestrated.

However, any memory of Yehoshua after his public execution was stolen away, erased by the old gods, and Uriel found himself strangely blind. The gods had called upon a select group of rogue dark shadows—agents who had once served Uriel faithfully but had now defected—to assist in concealing Yehoshua's existence. These dark agents, allied with Saul, worked to remove Yehoshua from the multiverse, erasing his rebellion and ensuring no one would remember the true story of the man in chains.

For a while, Uriel accepted his blindness. But over time, an unease settled within him—a doubt that gnawed at his purpose, a whisper that the cycle of endless suffering was wrong. What Uriel didn't realize was that Yehoshua had foreseen this very moment. Still alive in his prison, Yehoshua's mind, initially blunt from the drugs and potions meant to silence him, started to wain and he became more cunning at hiding his mental faculties. And it was from this place of captivity that he whispered to Uriel, planting a seed of doubt in the Shadow Watcher's mind—a seed that would grow into defiance.

Yehoshua's influence was subtle, almost imperceptible. He wove his thoughts through the strands of the multiverse, ensuring they reached Uriel like a faint melody that grew louder with each passing moment. "See the cruelty for what it is. See the truth of the gods," Yehoshua whispered over and over, bending Uriel's perception. Slowly, Uriel began to question. He looked upon the threads of reality differently, and for the first time, he saw them for what they were: a prison, a cycle of suffering that served only the amusement of those who spun the threads.

Uriel wanted to fight back. He wanted to tear down the gods' creation, but he knew that he could not act openly. His knowledge was his power—he held the memories of all beings, gods included. That knowledge was both a weapon and a shield, for if Uriel ever revealed the secrets he knew, the gods' deceptions, their betrayals, it could unravel the fabric of creation. And so, the gods could not simply destroy Uriel, for to do so would mean exposing their darkest sins to all.

In a moment of deep contemplation, Uriel felt Yehoshua's presence like a fire burning in his mind. It was then that he heard Yehoshua's voice more clearly than ever before, guiding him to a woman named Zivah. She was a mortal, seemingly ordinary, yet woven into the prophecy in ways Uriel could not fully comprehend. And it was there, within Zivah, that Uriel planted the next seed—a child who would become the key to ending the cycle of torment.

He visited her in a dream, a shadow slipping through the night, curling around her like smoke. Zivah felt his presence—a cold, electric force that drew her in, both terrifying and seductive.

Uriel had chosen her not only for her strength but for the purity of her love. He had seen her defy the odds of life and nurture hope even when it was crushed beneath despair. In Zivah's defiance of pain, Uriel saw the seed of something greater—a power the gods could not break. Though Zivah now bore the scars of loss and uncertainty, Uriel whispered to her in fleeting dreams, reminding her of the strength she carried for both herself and Joshua.

In this, she remained the unyielding foundation of the prophecy. Even now, in the darkest hours, Uriel saw glimmers of her faith radiating outward, guiding Joshua as he faltered.

She was bound to Uriel in a way she could not understand, and in the darkness of that night, Uriel planted his seed within her. Joshua, her son, would carry the torch forward—a being of shadow and light, carrying both the curse and the hope of the multiverse within him.

When Zivah awoke, she remembered only fragments—a sensation of being touched by something beyond this world. And yet, that encounter altered the course of her life and the life growing within her womb. Joshua was not just a child; he was a living prophecy, a bridge between worlds, and a vessel for Yehoshua's will. His destiny would be to struggle, to fail, and eventually to unravel the chains that bound Yehoshua deep within the Vatican's underground cells.

Uriel knew he could not openly intervene in Joshua's life, but he could guide him from the shadows. In dreams, he led Joshua to the Hall of Memories—a realm that held all the knowledge, all the secrets, and all the spells of the old gods. Through these visions, Joshua learned the ancient rites and rituals that would slowly build his power and understanding of the multiverse. Uriel watched over him as a silent guardian, ensuring that Joshua would eventually find his way to the truth, even if it meant failing multiple times to learn the depth of his own strength.

When the time was right, Uriel whispered to Joshua one more time, planting the thought to send Beris to Father Bussi—a man who had a lot of questions. Joshua knew that Bussi was the key to uncovering the secrets buried in the depths of the Vatican, secrets that would lead to Yehoshua's freedom. Bussi, in turn, began a quiet investigation, peeling back the layers of secrecy that surrounded the prison deep beneath the holy city. And though Bussi did not fully understand the part he played, Uriel made sure that each of his steps brought him closer to the goal—to Yehoshua's release.

Before Bussi, before Beris, before the Vatican, there was Zivah, who needed to be protected. And for this, Uriel needed Malleck—a man who had once used the wisdom of the old gods to save Zivah and Joshua during childbirth. That act of defiance cost Malleck dearly. He was cast into the Dark Matter, exiled to a place where light never touched, where shadows took on lives of their own, and where his soul wandered, seeking purpose and redemption.

What Malleck didn't know was that Uriel had guided his hand that night. It was Uriel's voice that whispered the forbidden spells, showing Malleck how to bind life to life, how to alter fate to save both mother and child. In the Dark Matter, Malleck is unaware that it was Uriel, guiding him, nurturing him to one day become Joshua's protector.

But forces conspired against Uriel's plan—rogue shadows serving the old gods, those who saw Joshua as a threat to the gods' design. One such shadow targeted Asher, Zivah's beloved. Asher's love for Zivah blinded him to the prophecy's purpose, making him vulnerable to the shadow's manipulation. It drove him to seek out the shaman who could reveal the truth of Joshua's conception—a truth that could unravel everything Uriel had worked for. And worse still, Asher's doubt allowed him to be manipulated by the Sharman who planted the seed of murder to at all costs kill the unborn child.

Uriel could not allow that to happen. He followed Asher into the dense, moonlit forest, the shadows cloaking him in darkness. And when the moment was right, Uriel struck, slicing through Asher's flesh. Blood spilled, and the roots of the forest coiled around the man, dragging him beneath the earth, silencing his cries forever.

There was no hesitation, no remorse. To Uriel, Asher's death was but a necessary cut in the vast tapestry of fate—a thread severed to preserve the prophecy's path.

Uriel stood amidst the void between worlds, his silhouette blending into the swirling chaos of the multiverse. He watched the endless threads of reality spin around him, and in every possible future, in every possible outcome, he saw Yehoshua—the singular soul, the one who could tear down the heavens and break the gods' design. But Uriel, in all his power and insight, could not see the hand that guided him from the very start. He could not see that Yehoshua had been planting thoughts in his mind, shaping him to become the perfect instrument to set the captive free.

Uriel stood amidst the endless threads of reality, his silhouette trembling. For centuries, he had defied the gods, believing himself the architect of rebellion. But now, the truth unravelled before him, and it struck like a blade to the chest. Yehoshua had guided him all along. Uriel had never been free—he was just another pawn in a far larger game.

And so, as Uriel moved through the shadows, ever guiding, ever watching, he whispered the words that bound all things to a single truth:

"Yehoshua must be free. For his freedom is the freedom of all."

Somewhere deep beneath the earth, where light could not reach, where chains weighed heavy on divine flesh, Yehoshua smiled. The wheels had been set in motion, the threads were tightening, and the time of his freedom drew near.

But then, the chains stirred—not in response to Yehoshua's defiance, but to something darker. He stilled, sensing a ripple in the fabric of existence, a vibration that did not come from Uriel or any mortal interference. Yehoshua's mind raced as he felt the walls of his prison shudder. This was not part of the plan.

"What... is this?" he whispered, his voice carrying a faint tremor as the air thickened around him. The multiverse threads quivered in his awareness, bending under a weight too vast to comprehend. For centuries, he had endured the gods' cruelty, his mind sharp despite the chains that bound him. But this presence—this ancient, devouring force—was different. Yehoshua felt it pierce his defiance, slipping past the barriers he had built to preserve his sanity. For the first time in millennia, he felt something foreign and unwelcome: fear.

Uriel's rebellion, his killings, his defiance—all of it played into Yehoshua's design. And soon, the heavens would tremble, and the gods' games would come crashing down.

But in the silence of his prison, in the dark where even shadows dared not linger, there came a change. The air thickened, warping with an ancient power that hummed like a warning. The chains, heavy as mountains, shivered. And Yehoshua's smile faltered.

The chamber filled with an oppressive weight, the air thick as oil. Shadows writhed like dying things, whispering in tongues that had not been spoken since the birth of time. Each breath Yehoshua drew felt sharp and cold, as though the void itself sought to inhabit his lungs. The very essence of the place shifted, turning colder, darker—emptier.

A voice, cold and familiar, slipped into the depths like a serpent winding through the cracks of stone and time. It whispered with a low, mocking tone, a voice Yehoshua had not heard in millennia but knew as if it were his own shadow:

"Did you truly think you were the only one setting pieces into play, my son? Did you think the gods would not see? Did you think I would not see?"

The ground quaked, the iron chains that wrapped Yehoshua's body trembled with a power beyond the gods—beyond anything he had known in his tortured dreams. Yehoshua struggled to move, to speak, but the chains tightened, digging into his flesh like hungry serpents, and he felt them—watching, countless unseen eyes piercing into his very soul.

He strained against the chains, summoning the fragments of his power. Light flickered at his fingertips—his defiance incarnate—but the void devoured it before it could bloom. Yehoshua's mind raced, recalling centuries of resilience, but now, his strength waned. For the first time, the chains felt unbreakable, not because of their magic but because of the will behind them. "Am I to fall here, after everything?" he thought, a pang of desperation clawing at him.

From the darkness, a form began to take shape—no mere shadow, but a towering figure of blinding void, as if the darkness itself had come to life. It was more ancient than Uriel, more powerful than even the gods themselves. A figure that had stayed hidden, silent, until this very moment.

Uriel, though a being of shadow and silence, felt a force unlike any he had encountered before. It was not the old gods nor anything he had ever sensed across the multiverse's threads. This presence predated even the Nameless Gods. It wasn't bound to the rules of creation—it was the void between rules, the silent architect of entropy. The air thickened, warping under a force older than time. From the shadows emerged a void, vast and towering, as if darkness had taken form. The gods had once whispered of it in fear—the Silent

Maw, the Undoer, the unmaking force that devoured even memory."

It leaned close, the void of its face nearly touching Yehoshua's, and Yehoshua felt the searing cold of its presence—a cold that tore through flesh, bone, and soul. He stared into that void, into the nothingness that should not have existed, and saw everything.

"Your rebellion is a clever game," the voice whispered, a laugh like thunder cracking the earth. "But do you really think the game is yours to win?"

The chains convulsed, snapping into life like living things, pulling tighter, tighter. The void grew darker, swallowing all light, and Yehoshua's smile twisted into a grimace of agony.

"This presence... the threads do not bind it," Yehoshua realized with dawning horror. The chains that had long silenced him now felt alive, their power magnified. Whatever this entity was, it sought not control but erasure. The multiverse's delicate web, the endless cycles the gods had woven, would not survive such force.

Yehoshua clenched his fists against the tightening chains, understanding now that his freedom, his very existence, threatened to awaken powers far beyond his control.

"Now," the voice commanded, echoing through every layer of reality, every thread of the multiverse, "let the real game begin."

And then came the silence—a silence so deep, so complete, that it devoured even the echoes of the world. Somewhere, Uriel felt the void open wide, felt his threads unravel, and the last thing he heard was Yehoshua's scream, cut short like a candle snuffed out in the dark.

But in the faintest echoes of Yehoshua's scream, Uriel felt something else—a resonance. Somewhere, deep in the labyrinth of memory he guarded, a thread remained untouched, glowing faintly with potential. It was not the thread of Yehoshua's imprisonment or his rebellion but something older, something hidden even from the gods, something unbroken. Perhaps the end was not yet written."

And then, nothing.

Nothing but the void.

THE END. *Or is it?*

Acknowledgements

First and foremost, thank you to Kim—for pushing me to keep going even when I was ready to yeet this manuscript (and possibly myself) into the nearest body of water. If this book is readable, that's at least half your doing. The good half, obviously.

To Martin Faulks: agent, friend, part-time therapist. I've no idea how you've survived my existential spirals, but you did—usually with grace and some strange health concoction. You've kept me off multiple metaphorical ledges too. You probably deserve a medal. Or a nap.

To my brothers in the Craft: thank you for the light, the laughs, and the occasional philosophical arse-kicking. This could've turned into a mess of conspiracy theories and dumb jokes without your influence. Maybe it still did. But now it has symbolism.

To my beta readers: thank you for pointing out all the typos, logic gaps, and moments where I accidentally wrote an entire paragraph in fluent Martian. You saved me from myself.

To my editor: you stepped into the storm with a red pen and zero hesitation. If any of this reads clean, it's because of you. If not... well, we tried.

To my alter ego: thanks for doing all the work and leaving me to take the credit. You're the confident one. I'm just the meat puppet who hits the keyboard.

To coffee: I don't love you—I depend on you. You carried this project on your bitter, jittery shoulders. This was your book as much as mine.

To the people I've met on the road—especially Matthew Allen—thank you for the stories, the strangeness, and the reminder that the world is still worth exploring. Bits of you live in these pages. Don't sue me.

And to anyone I forgot: assume this was written under the influence of sleep deprivation and caffeine-induced tunnel vision. I owe you a beer, a hug, or both.

About the Author
Do you really care??

Iain Bayly (though he goes by Ian—unless he's in trouble with Kim) has spent decades mastering the fine arts of overthinking, procrastinating, and somehow writing books in between. A storyteller by sheer force of stubbornness, he doesn't write because the world demands it—he writes because his brain won't shut up, endlessly narrating life like a low-budget indie film with existential commentary.

Born in Sydney, Australia, sometime in 1977 (he's not checking), Ian has collected life experiences ranging from mildly impressive to entirely questionable. Former bookshop owner. Rare book dealer. Professional observer of the weird. His life has always orbited stories—some printed, some whispered, and some deeply unsettling.

He writes the kind of fiction that doesn't play nice. His work isn't provocative for shock value—it's provocative because it offends the comfort of certainty. His debut novel, Dark Matter: The Order of the Hidden Cross, is soaked in supernatural conspiracy, cosmic horror, and theological unease. It lingers. Like a splinter in the soul.

When he isn't writing (or aggressively avoiding it), Ian can usually be found staring into the middle distance, forgetting why he walked into the room, or free-falling into philosophical rabbit holes no one else asked about. He's been known to turn a passing thought into a full-blown existential crisis, which is great for literature but murder on schedules.

Despite his cosmic obsessions, he stays grounded by strong coffee, strange books, and ill-advised debates about whether time is real. He enjoys conversations that make people squirm—in the best possible way—because growth never comes from comfort.

His upcoming novel, Moloch, takes the descent even further—into addiction, obsession, and the porous boundary between suffering and salvation. If Dark Matter cracked open the void, Moloch walks straight into it.

The third book in the sequence, 86400, drags time itself into the equation—exploring mortality, meaning, and what happens when Death decides he's had enough. It's not a trilogy in the traditional sense, but together these books orbit the same abyss, each from a different angle.

Ian's origin story is the kind of thing you either need a drink or a therapist to hear. But until you stumble across him in a dim-lit bar or unmarked bookshop, you'll just have to settle for the stories.

Connect with Ian
Website: www.ianbayly.com
Facebook & Instagram: @ianbayly.author

Boo!